A SECRET SUNRISE FOR THE COWGIRL

ELK MOUNTAIN RANCH BOOK FOUR

ELK MOUNTAIN RANCH

RUTH PENDLETON

V.2

CONTENTS

Chapter 1 1
Chapter 2 14
Chapter 3 27
Chapter 4 42
Chapter 5 55
Chapter 6 69
Chapter 7 81
Chapter 8 91
Chapter 9 101
Chapter 10 111
Chapter 11 122
Chapter 12 133
Chapter 13 144
Chapter 14 155
Chapter 15 165
Chapter 16 175
Chapter 17 185
Chapter 18 195
Chapter 19 205
Chapter 20 216
Chapter 21 227
Chapter 22 239
Chapter 23 249
Chapter 24 259
Epilogue 269

Also by Ruth Pendleton 281

CHAPTER 1

Hope Matthews walked onto the stage, microphone in hand, aware of the hundreds of eyes watching her. Years of practice had led to this moment. She was heading for her mark in the center of the stage when disaster struck. Hidden in the shadows was a small bead that had fallen off the previous performer's outfit. Gravity and timing were against Hope when she stepped on the bead and her feet went flying out from under her.

Instead of hearing the smooth lyrics of the song she wrote, the audience was treated to a loud shriek and then a thump when she fell backwards onto the ground. The microphone rolled to the side while Hope cradled her arm, furiously blinking back tears.

Hundreds of voice lessons and performing arts classes had given her the confidence to perform no matter how anxious she initially felt. But none of those classes had prepared her for the humiliation that came from sitting on her rear end in the middle of the stage, her left wrist throbbing fiercely.

The main lights to the auditorium flipped on and her friend Monroe thudded across the floor, his brown hair bouncing on his forehead while he ran. Not only was Hope in physical pain, but now she had to accept help from someone just to stand. Talk about a diva. If there were scouts in the audience, Hope was positive she had just ruined any hopes of them asking for a private meeting.

Rumors had been swirling all week that Ginny Brooks was looking for an act to open for her while she went on tour. It was the opportunity of a lifetime, and Hope wasn't going to miss it, no matter how badly her wrist hurt.

She shrugged off Monroe's help and reached for the microphone, biting her lip against the pain. "I've got it," she whispered. "Can you bring me a stand for the mic?"

Monroe knew better than to question her. Hope had proven, time and time again, that when she was determined to accomplish something, she was going to do it. That was why, probably against her better judgment, Hope found herself sliding the microphone into the stand, mustering a smile for the crowd.

"Well. How's that for a dramatic entrance?" Hope's nerves calmed as the audience gave a good-natured laugh. "I know you didn't come here to watch me fall flat on my rump. How about some music?"

She took a deep breath, steadying herself for the moment while the audience cheered. This was her chance to prove why she was one of the top students at the school. The first bars of music filled her veins with the courage she needed. She closed her gray eyes, keeping them shut while she sang the opening lyrics.

Hope's voice had been described as silky and smooth, with the sultry undertones of someone who understood love and pain. People sat back to listen to her music, getting caught up in the story of what she was singing about. The crowd in front of her was no different. Hope sang through to the final notes, letting her voice trail off.

The beat of silence before the audience burst into applause was something Hope lived for. She bowed, schooling her expression so the pain didn't show when she straightened up. The audience was still cheering when Hope left the stage, waving with her good hand. The second she was out of their sight, she burst into tears and fell into Monroe's open arms.

"You did it," he said. He had been Hope's best friend for years, seeing her through her share of botched auditions and amazing performances alike. She was now finishing her final semester of school before graduating with a master's degree.

Hugging Monroe with her good arm, Hope winced. "I think I'd better get to the doctor."

She had grown up on the ranch, with more spills and bumps and bruises than she could count. Between stitches on her shoulder from standing too close to a spooked horse to the giant bruise she carried for weeks after she fell off a ladder, Hope wasn't a stranger to pain.

The way her wrist felt, she wouldn't be surprised if it was broken.

The adrenaline was wearing off, and Hope knew she was moments away from collapsing. "Help me to my car?"

Monroe shook his head. "Sorry, Sunshine. There's no way you are driving yourself anywhere."

He was right. Hope leaned against his side. "So, how do you feel about a quick trip to the doctor's office?"

The world was starting to spin when Hope felt her feet leaving the earth. She was floating towards the door when she registered that Monroe had scooped her into his arms and was carrying her towards the parking lot like a small child.

She was vaguely aware of flashes of light when they paused outside Monroe's car. A fall like that would attract the attention of the school paper for sure. This wasn't the way Hope wanted to make the front page. Monroe jostled her while he muttered something about the keys, but then he was setting her in the seat.

Hope reached for the seatbelt, pulling it past her aching wrist so she could buckle it. She was aware of the purring of the car when it started, but she couldn't focus on anything Monroe was telling her. All she cared about was if she had performed well enough to get a callback.

It wasn't until he was pulling up in front of the urgent care clinic that Hope realized where Monroe was taking her.

"What about my doctor?" Hope asked.

Monroe shook his head. "I'm pretty sure you've broken

at least one bone. Your doctor's office might be able to set bones, but I didn't want to take the chance of them sending us away. We may as well start at the top."

Walking into the clinic took all of Hope's remaining energy. A receptionist brought a wheelchair out for her, and she gratefully sank down, cradling her arm in her lap. The waiting room had a few patients, but it wasn't long before they were calling Hope's name and Monroe was wheeling her back to a small examination room.

The nurse took her vitals before she left, promising that the doctor would be in soon. Hope waited until she left before she turned to Monroe.

"How badly did I bomb it?"

Monroe pulled her into a side hug, being careful not to jostle her arm. "Your audition?"

Hope grimaced. "Yeah. I know there's no chance Ginny Brooks will take me now, but that was also my final grade in Berry's class. Did I ruin my final semester of classes?" She leaned against her friend, grateful for the comfort he gave.

"What answer do you want? The one where I tell you that you could have laryngitis and still out sing most of the students in that class? Or the one where I tell you that falling flat on your rear end is something the school is going to gossip about until the next scandal comes along?"

"Remind me why we're friends, again?" Hope pushed her hair out of her face and studied Monroe's expression. He liked to tease her, but she knew he'd always tell her the truth.

"Because when you had your heart broken during the Spring Sing, I was the only one who saw what a jerk Cam had been. You know, that boba slushie I bought you was pretty much magic."

He was right. Her breakup sophomore year had led to one of the best friendships she had ever had. Five years later, Monroe had seen her through three other relationships and more than her fair share of emotions.

Hope closed her eyes. "I can't believe this happened. At least the day can't get any worse."

Monroe's eyes flew open. "You didn't just say that. Haven't you watched any medical dramas? It's as bad as saying good luck on opening night."

Hope patted his arm. "You are way too superstitious. I'm already injured. What else do you think will happen?"

Monroe shook his head. "I'm not sure, but the universe is creative. I'm sure it will come up with something."

The door opened and a portly man walked in. "Hope Matthews? I'm Doctor Jacobs. It's nice to meet you." He held his hand out to shake Hope's before pausing awkwardly. "Right. That isn't going to work for us, is it?"

"Nope." Hope's smile quickly fell when the doctor began his examination, reaching for her wrist.

"May I?"

She nodded. He was gentle when he softly felt down her arm, but every movement made her wince.

"Let's get some x-rays, and then we'll see what we're working with." He turned to his assistant. "Cayla, can you take care of that?"

Hope stood to walk, but Monroe pointed to the wheelchair. "Sit."

"I hurt my wrist. Not my foot." Hope frowned. "Besides, it's embarrassing having you wheel me around like I'm unable to walk."

Monroe scowled, his hand still out. "The last thing I need is you tripping over something else and hurting your other wrist. Please sit."

Hope sank to the chair, secretly appreciating the ride once they began to turn down a labyrinth of hallways. She glanced at Cayla. "Do you ever get lost in here?"

Cayla pointed to a square sign on the wall. "I got turned around all the time before they put these signs up. I think I could be half asleep now and still manage to find my way around. We're here."

The hallway opened into a small waiting area, with the lab on one side of the room and imaging on the other. A small girl sat cross-legged on one of the chairs in the corner, a book propped on her knees. Long, dark pigtails curled on either side of her neck. She glanced up when they entered but went back to reading her book.

A man was sitting next to the girl, his head tucked close to hers. As Monroe wheeled Hope past, she felt a sense of familiarity, like a wisp of memory she had somehow misplaced. His face was angled down towards the phone in his hands, and a baseball hat covered most of his dark hair, but there was something about him that tickled at the edge of her mind.

Monroe pushed her to the imaging side of the room,

where she bounced her leg up and down until her name was called. Until that moment, Hope had been pretty strong. That dissolved when the technician positioned her hand for each image, turning it in ways that sent waves of sharp pain through her body. She gritted her teeth, knowing it would be just a few minutes until the process was over. Then she would get answers.

The technician patted her arm when she was finished. "Sorry, hun. I know that wasn't fun. The doctor should have the images when you get back to the room."

"Thanks for your help." Hope sat in the chair, wiping away tears before she looked at Monroe. "Nothing like a good torture session to brighten the day."

Monroe started to wheel her through the waiting area, but he stopped at the drinking fountain. Hope was waiting for him to start moving when the lab door opened and a tall woman poked her head out. "Sierra?"

"It's your turn, Pumpkin."

The man's voice sent a shock wave through Hope. It had been seven years since she last heard him speak, but she would recognize that deep timbre anywhere. She twisted in the chair, looking back to see if the face matched the man in her memory.

They had been teens the last time Hope saw Silas. Time had added a chiseled jaw and a little scruff to his face, but the piercing blue eyes that slid past her with no recognition were the same ones Hope had spent years of her life fantasizing about.

Hope couldn't count the number of times she had

written his name on any surface she could find, including scratching it into the wood of her bunk bed. There was every variation she could think of, from the simple H + S, to writing *Mrs. Hope Foster* in fancy cursive letters across the front of her notebook.

Now he was walking the pig-tailed girl into the lab, and Monroe was wheeling Hope towards a long hallway. There were seconds left to say something, but her words were gone. What was she supposed to say to the man who broke her heart? He didn't just break it, but he stomped all over it and shredded it so badly, it took years for Hope to trust in love again.

She craned her neck as Monroe wheeled her away, watching the closed door until the last second to see if Silas was going to come back out. In a heartbeat she was gone around a corner, and the lab disappeared from sight. The pit in her stomach grew with every turn down the hallway until the nausea hurt worse than her wrist.

Monroe pushed her into the doctor's office, oblivious to the tsunami of emotions that were raging inside Hope's body. She was blinking furiously against a torrent of tears that simmered right beneath the surface. There was a time and a place to cry, but the doctor's office certainly wasn't it.

As Hope slid from the wheelchair to lean against the exam table, she jostled her wrist, and the dam broke. A torrent of tears fell to the tissue paper, leaving behind large splotches that wrinkled the paper.

She was aware of Monroe rubbing circles on her back,

trying to soothe her tears. All it did was make her cry even harder.

"I'm sorry, Sunshine." He pushed her hair to the side. "The doctor should be here any minute and we'll get some answers."

Hope knew he was trying to make her feel better, but there was nothing he or the doctor could do to ease the weight that was settling over her heart. Somewhere in the building was Hope's high school sweetheart. The way his eyes slid past her left no doubt that he had forgotten her completely.

She swiped at the tears, knowing it would do no good. "It's not the pain, although that definitely is a problem."

"Then what's wrong?" Monroe held out his hand and helped Hope to hop up on the exam table.

This was Hope's chance to tell him who she'd seen, but she was suddenly feeling shy. Monroe would take her side. That wasn't the question. The question was if she wanted to start talking about Silas, because once that door was open, she wasn't sure she'd be able to close it again.

She took a deep breath, trying to save the rest of her tears until she was tucked into her bed at home. Then she could have a good cry.

The door opened and the doctor came in, followed by Cayla. Their timing couldn't have been better. Dr. Jacobs tapped a few keys on his computer and pulled up the images on the screen.

"Well, Miss Matthews. I'm afraid today isn't your lucky day." He pulled a pen out from behind his ear and pointed to a couple of spots on the film. "See the lines here and here?"

Hope nodded. Even without a medical degree, the lines running horizontally across her bones were easy to see.

"This is what we call a transverse fracture. I'm afraid your arm is going to be out of commission for a few weeks."

He was being kind. Hope knew broken bones took a minimum of six weeks to heal. It was a good thing she was already planning a trip back home to the ranch for Bree's graduation. Her mom and little sister would spoil her while she recovered.

Dr. Jacobs opened a box and slid a padded splint out. "I'm going to need you to take it easy for the next few days." He gently slid the splint onto her arm, guiding her thumb through a small opening before he loosely secured the straps. "I need you to wear this day and night until the swelling goes down. Then we'll set the bone and put a cast on it."

"How long does it take for the swelling to go down?" Monroe stood to the side, his hands in his pockets.

Dr. Jacobs lifted Hope's arm into a sling, holding it in place while Cayla adjusted the straps around Hope's neck. "It usually takes five to seven days before we feel comfortable putting on the cast."

Hope looked at Monroe, knowing he was feeling helpless. "Hey. Finals are over. I'll be able to get caught up on all the shows I missed."

The smile he gave said he didn't believe her. "The Hope Matthews I know isn't capable of slowing down."

Dr. Jacobs glanced back and forth between them. "It really is important for you to be gentle. You don't want to injure yourself further."

Hope nodded. "He's just a worry wart. I'll be careful."

By the time the splint was properly placed, Hope was ready for the day to be over. She refused to sit in the wheelchair when they were leaving the office. "I'm not going to trip on the carpet, and even if I do, my arm is protected."

Monroe grunted but didn't say another word. Instead, he walked beside her, one hand resting firmly on her back in case she fell.

"How many years have you known me?" Hope looked at Monroe.

"I don't know. A million?"

Hope nodded. "Or five. And in those five years, have you ever seen me play the damsel in distress?"

Monroe shook his head. "You never know when that will start."

She grimaced but let Monroe lead her out to the parking lot. She knew how protective he could be.

They were pulling away from the urgent care clinic when Hope glanced back at the building. Silas stood in the window, his brow furrowed while he watched the car drive away. Whatever had happened in the doctor's office, Hope didn't think it was good news.

She turned her attention to Monroe. Silas was a figure

from her past, and that was where the memories of him needed to stay. She said a silent prayer that the girl Silas was helping was okay before she banished him to the farthest corners of her heart. Her life was here, in the present, with her best friend taking care of her. That was all that mattered.

CHAPTER 2

Silas stood in the waiting room of the urgent care clinic, his mind split in a million different directions. He had spent a long day with Sierra, waiting for the doctor to run test after test. Until a half hour ago, all Silas could focus on was his daughter, who had steadily been losing weight no matter what he fed her.

He hadn't been paying attention when a couple walked into the lab. Doctor's visits should be private. It wasn't his business why someone else would need help so he had kept his head down, playing a word game on his phone while he and Sierra waited.

Everything would have been fine, except he looked up when the nurse called Sierra's name and found himself staring at a ghost from the past. Silas had dated his fair share of women, but there was only one woman who haunted his dreams. Hope Matthews.

Now, a half hour later, she was leaving the doctor's

office with a man who clearly loved her. There was a sling hanging from Hope's shoulder, and Silas involuntarily reached for his phone. Years ago, he would have texted her immediately to make sure she was okay. It wasn't his place now. She had a muscular, brown-haired man helping her walk to the car. She didn't need a phone call from an ex.

She wouldn't answer anyway. People liked to say that there were always two sides to every relationship, but he knew that breaking up with Hope was all on him. The reasons back then were complicated, but Hope didn't know that.

A small hand tugged at Silas's shirt, snapping his attention back to the present. "Can we go home yet, Daddy?"

Silas knelt down and flicked one of Sierra's ponytails. "Almost. I need to make your next appointment and then we can go get a treat."

"Ice cream?" Sierra was bouncing on her toes.

"Yep. Ice cream with chocolate and sprinkles." Silas loved how excited his daughter was. He'd buy her all the ice cream in the world if it would help her to get better.

His name was called, and he headed to the receptionist to set up an appointment for the following week. Pam leaned over the desk and called Sierra to her. "Do you want a sticker?"

Sierra's eyes lit up. "Yes, please. Thank you."

"Take care of your dad, this week, okay?" Pam was Silas's favorite receptionist. She knew how difficult it was to be a single parent to a sick child. He was sure she paid special attention to Sierra whenever Silas brought her in.

"See you next week, Pam."

Silas headed towards the parking lot, where his mind immediately flashed back to the sight of Hope climbing into a car, her man holding the door open for her until she was settled. He felt a twinge of jealousy. The look of gratitude she gave the man left no doubt that she was happy in her relationship. The love was evident there.

Silas held Sierra's hand while they walked to the car, gently swinging it back and forth. Finding out that he was going to be a dad at nineteen had been the worst news of his life. He was a senior in high school, dating Hope, and looking forward to building a future with her. His ex-girlfriend, Zoe, hadn't told him she was pregnant until the end of the year, when she decided she was going to run away from home.

The worst day of his life turned into the biggest blessing. Silas couldn't imagine life without his sweet Sierra in it. If anything, the past seven years had taught him to appreciate all the little things most people missed, from slowing down to watch a butterfly flitting between flowers to laughing in the rain.

They reached the car and Silas pulled Sierra's door open. "Hop in."

Sierra climbed into her booster seat and immediately began tapping her feet against the seat in front of her.

"Am I doing the buckle or are you?" Silas waited for his answer. He knew better than to fasten the seatbelt before Sierra was ready. The last thing he needed was her sulking because he had done the buckles wrong.

"Your turn," she said. She reached for her cup, taking a sip of water. "I didn't like that doctor."

Silas nodded. "I don't like getting my blood drawn either. You were so brave though."

Sierra rubbed the Band-Aid on her arm. It was covered with different colored ponies. "Did they give you a Band-Aid when they poked you?"

"Yes, but not a cute one. Which one is your favorite pony?" Silas stood by the door, waiting for Sierra to make her decision.

"I like the pink one." She pointed to a pony that was standing on two legs.

"Ooh. That's a good one." Silas kissed the top of Sierra's head before closing her door. His shoulders were weighed down while he walked to his side. Having a child was difficult in any circumstance, but handling health scares without a partner to help? That was a lot for one man to deal with while trying to juggle work and home responsibilities.

Sierra's mom, Zoe, had been in the picture for the first three years of her life. Silas became her full legal guardian when his ex was found convulsing from a drug overdose at a local park. Paramedics had worked hard to save Zoe's life, but that was the final straw for Silas. He fought and won the right for Sierra to have a stable home with her dad.

He had done his best to shield Sierra from the ugly side of her mom's addiction. The following year, when Zoe lost her battle against drugs, Silas was truly on his own.

He tried to fill the roles of both mom and dad so Sierra

didn't feel cheated out of anything life had to offer. He watched hair styling tutorials so she had cute hair. He bought dress up shoes and t-shirts with kittens on them. He gave her sparkles and stuffed animals.

From the outside, Sierra looked like all the little girls in her first-grade class. It was the inside that was different. Her class didn't see the nights Sierra cried herself to sleep, clutching her stomach in pain.

Silas was afraid he wasn't going to be able to find the answers he needed. So far, the doctors hadn't been able to come up with a reason for her pain or the weight loss. Silas clicked his seatbelt, praying that this time, the blood results would show something they could treat.

He checked the rear-view mirror, where Sierra was happily humming to herself. She met his eyes and Silas winked. "Who's ready for ice cream?"

"Me!" Sierra crossed her arms in front of her. "Do I get one or two scoops?"

Silas backed out of the parking spot. "How about one for being good at the doctor, and an extra one for getting your blood drawn?"

"Yay!" Sierra wriggled back and forth in her seat. Her excitement was contagious.

"Alright. Two scoops for my favorite girl."

By the time Silas was wiping rainbow sherbet off of Sierra's chin, all thoughts of the Hope sighting were pushed out of his mind. He had his daughter to focus on. Even if Hope were single, which she clearly was not, there wasn't room in his life for a relationship. His daughter was his priority.

After an evening of playing princess and the dragon, which involved him crawling across the floor and roaring at Sierra, Silas tucked her into bed. He read her two stories, and then, because she had been so good for the doctor, he read her a third.

"Time for prayers," he said.

Sierra knelt on her bed. "Heavenly Father. Thank you for my dad. Please bless my tummy to get better and bless my dad that he can find me a mom."

Silas's eyebrows shot up, but he kept his eyes closed. That was a new request.

"Thank you for Grandma and Grandpa and Coco and Simmy. In Jesus name, amen."

"Amen." Silas kissed both of Sierra's cheeks. "One kiss for good dreams, and one kiss to keep the monsters away."

Sierra held out her stuffed monkey. "What about Coco?"

Silas kissed each of the monkey's soft cheeks and then tucked him beside Sierra when she snuggled into her covers.

"Don't forget Simmy."

The patched brown and white striped cat was missing from the bed. Silas felt along the floor, knowing the cat wouldn't be far. Sure enough, he found it tucked near the foot of the bed.

"Two kisses for Simmy." He tucked the cat on the other

side of Sierra, bending down to kiss her forehead. "And one final kiss to remember I love you."

"Goodnight, Daddy." Sierra yawned, covering her face with her hand.

"Goodnight, Pumpkin."

Silas headed to the hallway where he sat outside Sierra's door. He wanted to be close if she started to cry. Fifteen minutes later he poked his head in, his heart taking comfort at the sight of her chest raising and falling with each deep breath.

The doctor had asked Silas to begin tracking when Sierra had good nights and when she had bad nights. Silas pulled out his phone and jotted a quick note. This was a good night, which they both needed. He headed to his bedroom at the other end of the hall and closed the door. He'd open it a crack when he went to bed, but for now, he didn't want to accidentally wake Sierra up.

Silas flipped on the tv, mindlessly scrolling from one channel to the next. There was never anything good to watch. He settled for the recap of yesterday's NBA playoffs game. Silas's favorite team had gotten eliminated early in the tournament. He wasn't invested in who was going to win now, but the highlight reel lifted his spirits. This was what he thought his life would look like, except in his dreams, a woman would be snuggled up by his side cheering with every shot that went in.

Unbidden, Hope sprung to mind. She hadn't been his first girlfriend, but she was the only one he had dreamed of marrying one day. He was glad she seemed to be happy. In high school she was a friend to everyone. It didn't surprise him that she had found someone to live her life with.

Silas was brushing his teeth when his phone rang. He stifled a groan when he saw the caller ID. His mom always meant well, but Silas didn't want to rehash the doctor's visit. He hated constantly telling her that yes, the visit went well. No, they didn't get any new answers. And no, he wasn't sure what the next step should be.

He ignored the ringing and let the phone go to voicemail. A phone call in the morning on his way to work wouldn't change the answers, but it would give Silas a limited amount of time to talk before his mom would have to let him go. There was a flicker of guilt as the phone fell silent, but Silas knew his limits. He was already tapped out for the day.

THE STOMACHACHE that Silas had been expecting Sierra to have the previous night hit in the morning when she was getting ready for school. He was braiding her hair when she bent over, clutching her stomach.

Silas paused, holding the brush mid-air. "Are you okay, Pumpkin?"

"I'm okay, Daddy. I'll be okay at school." Sierra's brown eyes filled with tears when she tried to straighten up.

Silas smoothed his features so he looked calm and reassuring. It took a great effort to keep a smile on his face when he felt like shouting in frustration. Surely someone, somewhere could figure out why his baby girl was in so much pain.

"How about we ditch today?"

Sierra's little head waggled back and forth. "I don't want to. It's our pizza party today to celebrate doing our reading charts. I can't miss it."

The temptation to send Sierra to school was strong. Silas had already taken half the day off to take her to the doctor the day before. He could do his work from home, but it was much more difficult to work without the team in the office. The camping season was already in full swing, and as a civil engineer for the forest service, he was thick in the middle of making sure all the facilities were running how they needed to be.

Silas pulled his daughter into a hug. "That sounds like a lot of fun. I'm sorry your tummy isn't cooperating today."

The waterworks were beginning in earnest, even though Sierra tried to wipe the tears away. "It isn't fair. Why do I always have to miss the fun things?"

The ropes cinching into knots in Silas's stomach were familiar. He felt the heaviness of the situation pressing down on him. Not only was he failing to take care of his daughter physically, but now he was failing to take care of her emotionally. There had to be a solution, but it evaded him no matter how hard he looked. The knots holding him down cinched tighter.

He glanced at his phone when it began to ring and held back a sigh. For the second time in as many days, he sent his mom to voicemail. The call to her was going to have to wait a little longer.

"I have an idea." Silas headed to the kitchen and opened a drawer, pulling out a stack of paper and a box of crayons. "How about we have our own party today?"

Sierra's eyes widened. "We can't do that."

"Why not?"

She pointed to Silas's computer bag. "Because you have to go to work, and I want to go to school." Even as she spoke, she was curling into a ball with her hands pressed against her stomach.

"Sorry, Pumpkin. It looks like the tummy goblins are winning today. The good news is that we get to spend the day together. We can order whatever you want for lunch and have our own party. Deal?"

Sierra gave a hesitant nod, her lips pressing together. "Can we get pizza?"

"Only if you let me eat your crusts."

That earned a giggle from Sierra. "That's the yucky part. I don't want them."

Silas grinned. "Do you want to color for a little bit while I check in with work?"

Sierra slid off her chair with the crayon box in one hand and the papers in the other and headed towards the family room. "I'm going to color a unicorn."

"I can't wait to see it."

Silas waited until Sierra turned the corner before he sank into the wooden chair. The glass of the tabletop was smooth against his arms where he clasped his hands. He took a minute to collect his thoughts, and then he began to pray. His voice wavered at first as he begged the Lord to help him find answers. Then he trailed off. What was the point in praying to a God who didn't seem to listen?

He was supposed to be strong enough to care for his daughter, but Silas didn't know how to do that on his own. No amount of research could help him take away her pain. Instead, he got a front row seat to see how strong of a girl she was. Sierra was incredible.

Silas pulled out his phone and listened to the messages from his mom. The first one was asking about Sierra's appointment. The second one surprised Silas. He glanced at his work computer and then called his mom back. Work could wait.

"Hi mom. I just have a few minutes."

"Is she having another hard day?" Silas's mom had always been perceptive.

"We're hanging out at the house." He knew his mom would want to fix everything, but she couldn't.

"I see. Did you listen to my messages?"

Silas rubbed the bridge of his nose, trying to remain calm. "I did."

"So, what do you think? Do you want to bring Sierra home for a visit? She could play with her cousins."

His mom had been asking a variation of the same question for the past couple of years. It was understandable that she'd want to spend time with her granddaughter. Silas had even been considering it, but there was never a convenient time to drive Sierra home. Then she got sick. There was no way Silas could let her go alone.

He clasped his hands together. "Mom, she's sick. Until we figure out what is happening, I don't think that is a good idea."

"School ends in a few weeks. Maybe she could come for part of the summer."

His mom made it sound so easy. Just drop Sierra off and hope someone would notice when she was in pain. Forget the doctors visits and time he'd have to take off. "I can't do that, Mom."

There was a brief pause. "What if you stay with her?"

That invitation had been extended before as well, but Silas didn't want to go home. In the small town where gossip flowed freely, Silas knew what his reputation was. He was the kid who strayed from the church teachings and got a young girl pregnant. Everyone had their struggles, but the pregnant ex-girlfriend was difficult to hide.

A lot of people dreamed of going home, but not Silas. He didn't need eyes watching him as he walked around town with his daughter. They could judge Silas all day, but he would shield Sierra from the gossip as long as he could.

"Mom. We've talked about that. It isn't a good time to visit."

His mom interrupted him. "Honey, I am worried about you. I know being a single dad is a lot of work. Why won't you let me help?"

Silas smacked his fist on the table. "We're doing fine

over here." He rubbed his hand, trying to keep his voice steady. "I have a meeting I need to get to. We'll talk later."

He hung up the phone before giving his mom a chance to say goodbye. Logically, he knew she was trying to help. In reality, all she was doing was adding another complication to his life.

Silas opened his computer, checking his emails before he joined the video call with the rest of his team. His heartbeat steadied as he discussed trail erosion with his coworkers. By the time the meeting was over, he was feeling much better.

He wandered to the family room to check on Sierra. She looked up with a smile.

"I drew hearts, Daddy." The paper she held up was covered with a layer of hearts, each one a different color.

"Great job, Pumpkin. They look great."

Sierra beamed. She handed the picture over and reached for a new piece of paper. "Are we going to go visit grandma?"

Silas should have known Sierra would eavesdrop on his conversation. He opened his mouth to say no, and then paused.

"Do you think you'd like that?"

Sierra nodded so enthusiastically, her braids swung back and forth. "Yeah. I want to see Grandma and Grandpa."

Maybe it would be the break they both needed. "Alright. I'll see what I can do."

CHAPTER 3

The first thing Hope noticed when she climbed out of the car was the smell of fresh cut hay. She breathed in deeply. Whenever she got the whiff of a ranch, she was immediately transported back home. Now she was here, breathing the air that had formed much of her childhood.

Monroe climbed out of the car, stretching his hands above his head before leaning from side to side. He folded over, his hands a foot away from touching the ground and then he straightened up.

Hope tried to hold back a smile. "Thanks again for coming home with me. You didn't have to do that."

Monroe clasped his hands behind his back and pulled them away from his body in another stretch. "It's not that long of a drive. Okay. Maybe five hours is long, but now I get to see where the infamous Hope Matthews lives."

"I can't believe that you never came here on any of our college breaks. You were certainly invited."

"My mom would have been sad. She and my dad are still trying to figure out life as empty nesters."

Hope walked to the back of the car, reaching for her backpack. "I'm not sure my mom will have to deal with that for a while. Especially not with Thomas and Hazel moving into their house on the property. It's not the same as them living with her, but they're close enough to do family dinners."

Monroe walked back to where she stood, and his jaw dropped. "What do you think you are doing?"

"I broke one arm. Not both of them. I can handle my backpack." Monroe hadn't stopped fussing over her since she had fallen three weeks ago.

"I know, but how am I supposed to impress your mom if I'm letting her injured daughter carry things?" His expression was so serious, Hope burst into laughter.

"Fine." She handed the backpack over and stepped back. If Monroe wanted to be her pack mule, who was she to say no? There would be more suitcases to carry in once she knew where Monroe was going to be sleeping.

She led him up the stairs into the house, pausing in the entryway to shout. "I'm here. Where's my hug?"

There was a thundering of feet on the stairs and Bree rounded the corner, running full speed until she was close to Hope. Then she skidded to a stop, her feet sliding an extra couple of inches.

"I forgot I can't tackle you." Bree gently wrapped her arms around Hope's waist, giving her a hug. "I missed you."

Hope tousled her hair. "Me too. I haven't seen you since Christmas."

"It's been forever." Bree's words were muffled because she was speaking into Hope's shoulder.

Hope rubbed Bree's back until she let go. "Sis, I want you to meet my friend Monroe."

Monroe held his hand out, but Bree pushed past it, giving him a hug. "It's good to meet you. Hope says you've been helping her out."

"She doesn't want to admit it, but I'm pretty good at taking care of her. At this point, though, I think I've moved past friends to unofficial chauffeur." He winked at Hope.

"Just because you drove me home–"

"And to and from the doctor. Twice. And around town to get groceries. And to the gas station to fill up your car."

Hope bumped Monroe with her hip. She looked at Bree. "Okay. I couldn't have done any of that without him."

"It's our turn to take care of Hope now." Bree reached for Hope's good hand and pulled her towards the kitchen. "Mom is out in the garden planting the rest of the tomatoes, but she said I had to tell her when you guys got here."

"Where is everyone else?"

The ranch was usually bustling with people, from family members to the employees that Mom Matthews had recently hired to help offset her sons getting married.

"Reid is out in the fields, although Millie promised

she'd come by for dinner. You'll for sure see him then if he doesn't come in sooner." Bree grinned. "I think he's going to propose to her soon, but whenever I ask, he changes the subject."

Hope bit the side of her cheek to hide a smile. She had seen the way Reid acted around his girlfriend. Everyone would be shocked if they weren't engaged before the end of the year. Millie was the best thing to ever happen to Reid.

Bree continued on, oblivious to Hope's thoughts. "Porter and Emily will probably swing by for dinner. They have some big news to share." She gasped and clasped her hand over her mouth. "Except I wasn't supposed to tell you that. Please act super surprised when they make their announcement."

In Hope's experience, there weren't a lot of surprises that married people had to tell. They could announce a move or a career change, but Emily's llama center was doing a lot of good in the community. She couldn't see Emily wanting to leave that any time soon. And Porter still helped out on the ranch almost every day.

That left the news Hope had been waiting for since both of her brothers got married. She had been counting the days until one of them announced that they were pregnant. Hope was going to be the best aunt ever, spoiling her little niece or nephew rotten.

She smiled at her sister. "I won't tell them you said anything." She glanced at her watch. There were still a few hours until dinner. The suspense was going to do her in. She headed towards the back door.

Bree continued her rundown of the family while Monroe followed behind. "Thomas and Hazel are probably in the barn. Sunflower is sick again."

Hope stopped walking. "How sick?" That horse was one of her favorite things that reminded her of her dad. She had learned to ride on Sunflower, laughing as her dad led her around the pasture.

"It's nothing bad. Hazel says it's just a cold. Anyway, we can go see them next." Bree reached for her arm, pulling her along.

Walking arm in arm with Bree was similar to walking with a tornado. She talked a mile a minute, throwing out so much information, Hope was struggling to keep up. She glanced at Monroe, who was keeping pace behind them. They exchanged glances and he gave her a wry grin.

Monroe cleared his throat. "Remind me how many siblings you have?" He was directing his question towards Hope, but Bree cut in.

"There are eight of us. Porter, Thomas and Reid are all here, but Hudson, Finn and Wyatt are off doing their own things. I'm headed to college in the fall so I'll get to see the twins more often."

Hope glanced at Monroe. His furrowed eyebrows made it look like he was memorizing facts for a test. Early on in their friendship, Monroe had asked about her family. Hope had been reluctant to talk about them much. It made her too homesick. Instead, their conversations revolved around music, auditions, and where the future would lead.

"Finn and Wyatt are the twins. They turn twenty-one this year." Bree had gone through a brief period of depression when they headed to college a few years back. Hope was excited for her sister to join them at school in the fall.

They reached the back fence. Bree pushed open the gate and Hope followed after her. She glanced at Monroe. "Are you doing okay?"

He nodded. "I'm excited to meet the mom of my most famous friend."

Fields of grass sprawled beyond the fence. Large, raised garden boxes stood off to the side. Hope stopped to take in the view. In the winter, the ground would be covered with snow, making for harsh conditions. Once the snow gave way to new growth, the ranch became a beautiful place.

Hope spotted a figure bending over in the distance. "Hi Mom," she yelled, waving with her good arm.

Her mom straightened up, wiping her hands on her apron before running towards Hope.

"You made it!"

Hope leaned into her mom's hug, blinking back tears. She had been brave when she broke her arm, but truth be told, she was physically and emotionally exhausted. She was sure she had bombed any chance at a callback for The Ginny Brooks band, and her body was sore from having to use different muscles to compensate for the broken arm.

"I missed you." Hope gave her mom an extra squeeze

and then stepped back. "Mom, I'd like you to meet Monroe."

"It's a pleasure to meet you, Ms. Matthews." Monroe stretched his hand out but Mom Matthews brushed it away, wrapping her arms around him.

"We do hugs here. Everyone is a friend."

Monroe met Hope's eyes once again, his expression difficult to decipher. Hope had forgotten that her family could be a lot to get to know all at once. She didn't have time to check in with him though, because Thomas and Hazel were heading their way.

After a new round of hugs and introductions, Hope found herself standing near Hazel. Hazel leaned in to rest her head on Hope's shoulder. "How are you holding up?"

Hope knew her sister-in-law wanted an honest answer. Hazel took care of animals all day. As a vet, she was used to assessing pain.

"It's been a little more difficult than I imagined, but I'm doing okay." Hope held up her arm. "Besides, now I have a nifty cast everyone can sign."

Hazel looked her up and down. Perhaps she noticed the tears brimming in Hope's eyes because she didn't push it further.

"We're glad you're home." Thomas stepped forward to give Hope another hug. She had missed him.

"How is the new house?" The last time Hope had been home, the barn conversion was well underway. There had still been several things to finish though. Now it was complete, and the happy couple had moved in a couple of months ago.

Thomas grinned at his wife. "It's perfect for us."

Hazel nodded. "Do you want to come see it?"

The idea was tempting, but Hope shook her head. "We need to get settled first, and then I need a snack. I'd love to come by later."

"I can't wait to show you around." Hazel reached for Thomas's hand. "It really is the best."

Mom Matthews reached out and pulled a piece of hay off of Thomas's shirt before she turned to Hope. "Let's get you settled." She began to walk towards the house, with the kids trailing behind.

Hope reached for Monroe's shoulder, holding him back. She waited until the family was out of earshot before speaking. "How are you handling the chaos of my family so far?"

Monroe's eyes were sincere when he answered. "It is always refreshing to be around people who genuinely love each other. I can tell you guys are happy being together."

"We are, but that doesn't mean they aren't overwhelming." Hope was worried that Monroe was so focused on taking care of her, he wasn't going to speak up if he needed something.

He brushed her hair back. "Hope, your family is perfect. I'm glad I could finally meet them."

She leaned against his side. "You're my best friend. I have to make sure I am taking care of you, too."

He rolled his eyes and pulled her towards the house. "How are you going to take care of me? You're half my size."

Hope flexed her arm, showing off a small mound of muscles. She laughed. "I'll take out anyone who tries to mess with you. If my muscles give out, I've been told I do a pretty mean hair flip."

The warm sun beat down on their backs while they walked. Hope's world felt complete with Monroe finally taking part of it. He fit on the ranch in a way she hadn't expected.

"Alright. You win. If I need something, I'll ask you to get it for me. Or, if all else fails, you can toss your hair. That should fix everything."

Hope reached for his hand, giving it a squeeze. "How's your heart today?" For as much bravado as Monroe put on, he wasn't in the best of head spaces after a horrible breakup the month before. She was worried that he was ignoring his own feelings to take care of her.

Monroe looked away. "I think I'm still in shock. I mean, I knew Mandy and I weren't going to make it for the long haul, but I didn't expect her to dump me so publicly."

The vision of Monroe standing in the center of campus, surrounded by students, was one she'd never forget. Mandy had been yelling so loudly, a security officer came to assist. He escorted Mandy away, leaving behind a stunned Monroe. Hope barely made it to his side before he sank to the ground, bowing his head in defeat.

"I was there. She looked way worse than you. I'm guessing that when people gossip about the breakup, they're going to mention the screaming girl. Not the man who took her abuse without flinching."

"I would never yell back."

"I know. That's why I wouldn't worry about your reputation. I know that was hard for your heart, though."

They headed across the lawn to the back door where Mom Matthews was waiting. "Monroe, I'm going to put you in Porter's old room. We turned that into a guest room. And Hope, you know where to go."

Hope glanced at Monroe. He wore a shadow across his face, like he was trying to keep his emotions together. Maybe it had been a bad idea to ask about his ex. Mandy hadn't been one of Hope's favorite choices for Monroe, but overall, she had been a decent girlfriend until the breakup. "Thanks, Mom. That sounds perfect. I'll show him where to go and then we'll come down to eat."

She led Monroe out the front door, giving him a minute to gather his thoughts. Monroe gave her hand a grateful squeeze once they were standing by the car. "Thanks. I needed that. Thinking about Mandy always puts me in a bit of a funk."

"I shouldn't have brought her up." Hope hugged him with her good arm. "I'm sorry."

Monroe rested his chin on her head. "Honestly, your family seems great. I'm glad I came."

"Me too." Hope knew Monroe was trying to take care of

her, but she hoped some good ranch air would help him to heal as well.

He had perked up by the time they were done putting away their suitcases. Hope was sitting at the table, munching on a bowl of chips and homemade salsa when the kitchen door banged open. Reid strolled into the kitchen, tossing a nod over his shoulder. "Hey, Hope. What's up?"

She smirked as he held his hands under the faucet. Trust Reid to not notice the tall man sitting next to her. Sure enough, he was scrubbing his hands when he froze and slowly turned to look over his shoulder. Reid's poker face was hard to read, but Hope knew the pieces were clicking into place.

He slowly turned, taking his time to dry his hands on a towel before sauntering over to the table. "Hi there. Reid Matthews."

Monroe shook his hand. "I'm Monroe."

Thomas lifted his chin with a quick nod. "It's nice to meet you. How long have you been dating my sister?"

A stream of water spewed from Hope's mouth while she tried to answer. Instead of forming words, she sputtered and coughed, trying to clear her airway.

Monroe beat her to the punch. "We're not dating. We're just friends."

"Uh huh." Reid handed the towel over to Hope. "Millie and I weren't dating either. And now we've been together almost a year."

Hope's airway was finally clear. She tossed the towel to

the floor, kicking it to the side of the table. "I met Monroe my sophomore year of college. He's helped me through some difficult times, but we have never dated. You know it's possible to have friends of the opposite gender, right?"

Reid grinned. "Yeah, but it's so much more fun if I can tease you about it." He tucked his hands in his pockets and headed for the door.

"Bye, Reid." Hope waited until he was almost to the door. Then she raised her voice in an exaggerated whisper. "And there goes my least favorite brother."

Reid turned, giving a mock bow. "I'll see you at dinner time."

Monroe laughed, taking the ribbing in stride. "I can imagine how fun it was growing up with three older brothers."

"Four. Hudson is older than me as well."

"Oof. Even worse."

Bree came into the kitchen. "What is worse?"

"Growing up with four older brothers." Hope grinned. "But you had to deal with six older brothers and one incredible older sister."

"I'm pretty lucky." Bree swiped the last chip out of the bowl. "What are your plans for the rest of the day?"

Hope exchanged glances with Monroe. She hadn't thought that far ahead when she invited him to come home for a visit. "I guess we could put him to work."

Monroe cocked an eyebrow. "As in, ranch work?"

Bree was starting to bounce on her toes. "Do you want to help me muck out the barn?"

Hope nodded enthusiastically. "He would love that. What do you say?"

Monroe held out his hands. "As you can see, these hands weren't made for farm work. See the lack of calluses? That's because I've chosen the much more manly career of singing."

Bree's bouncing slowed. "Wait. You're a singer too? Like Hope?"

"I want to be. My problem is breaking into the business." Monroe traced the grain lines along the top of the table. I've gotten rejected more times than I can count."

"Don't let him fool you." Hope nudged him in the side. "He's one of the best performers I know."

Bree planted her hands on her hips, looking him up and down. "I don't know. I bet you'd make a pretty cute cowboy." She turned on her heels and headed for the back door. "I'll be in the barn if you change your mind."

Monroe's face had turned a bright shade of red. "Is your little sister hitting on me?"

"That's just the way she is. She's never been afraid to say what was on her mind, even when her friends would tease her about it."

"Well, I'm glad to know I'm cute. If my music fails, I guess I'll be getting a career over here, mucking out barns."

That triggered an idea. Hope slid her chair back from the table. "Come with me."

Monroe followed her to the front room, watching as she pulled out a stack of photo albums. By the time she had shown him some of her worst pictures, he was smiling again. The day hadn't been a total bust.

Hope was pulling out another album when her stomach began to flip. This album held her high school years. "I've bored you enough for one day." She moved to close the album, but Monroe's hand shot out.

"No way we're stopping now. I want to see your bad hair styles and goofy clothes."

Hope took a breath and nodded. The first half of the scrapbook brought back a lot of good memories. It was as they flipped through the later pages that Hope's heart began to sink. That was where group pictures began to show up. Before long, Silas appeared frequently, with a cheeky grin plastered across his face and his arm around her waist.

Hope thought she was over him. She had successfully put Silas out of her mind and been able to have fulfilling relationships. But seeing him at the doctor's office had opened a carefully guarded spot in her heart. He was the only guy to leave her with no explanation. One minute he was there. The next, he was ghosting her like they'd never met.

Each page brought back another wave of memories until Hope felt like she was going to drown. She closed the book. "Sorry, Monroe. I can't look at those."

He must have seen something in her expression because he didn't press it. Instead, he took the book from her hands and placed it back on the shelf. "Do you want to talk about it?"

Hope met the eyes of her best friend. They told each other everything, but these memories were too complicated to share. "Not yet."

By the time Mom Matthews was calling everyone in for dinner, Hope had carefully tucked Silas back away. She had loved him with all her heart, and he had rejected her. He didn't deserve any more of her thoughts.

CHAPTER 4

Sierra fell asleep two hours into the drive home, leaving Silas alone with his thoughts. With each passing mile, he could feel the pressures of home weighing more heavily on his heart. He would have gladly skipped the entire trip if it wasn't for the little girl snoozing against her booster seat's headrest.

She had been talking non-stop about going home to see Grandma and Grandpa Foster. It was the first thing Sierra had been truly excited about in a long time. Silas was willing to deal with any amount of discomfort if it made his daughter happy.

The visit would make her smile, and that was all that mattered.

Fifteen miles outside of town, Silas's heart began to race. He had forgotten how many memories were crammed into one small town. He passed a large billboard with a picture of a cow holding a giant ice cream cone. "Elk Mountain's famous ice cream, next exit."

The Spotted Cow Diner was top on his list of places to take his ice-cream-loving daughter. He couldn't wait to see her eyes light up.

The emotions slammed into him a mile later. The Spotted Cow diner was where he had gone on his first date with Hope. Ever since seeing her at the urgent care clinic, he couldn't get her out of his mind. The only good thing about leaving the city was that he was leaving her behind. He didn't have to worry about running into her back at home.

Two miles outside of town, Silas reached his arm back and gently rubbed Sierra's knee. "We're almost there, Pumpkin."

Sierra yawned and rubbed her eyes. "I get to see Grandma and Grandpa?"

"Yes. They are waiting to give you a giant hug."

Silas had to give his parents credit. They hadn't understood why their eighteen-year-old son was suddenly spending all his time in his room, or why he refused to take the phone calls of his girlfriend. All they knew was that he was hurting.

He could never forget his mom's face when he slammed the door on his way out of town. Zoe had decided to move to the city to have the baby. So far, only a few people knew she was expecting. If she left right away, no one would ask about the baby bump.

Following the woman he was no longer in love with took a lot of guts, but he wasn't going to be a deadbeat dad who ignored his responsibilities. If Zoe was moving to the city, so was he. He had turned nineteen a few months later, with no family or friends around to celebrate. Holding Sierra after she was born made every sacrifice worth it.

He turned the car down a two-lane street, swallowing back the uneasiness that was crawling over his skin. The houses looked the same as he remembered, but there were slight changes. He was looking at them through a new lens, and now he was much more observant.

There were no cars behind Silas. This was a good thing when he slowed to a stop in the middle of the road. He needed to take a few cleansing breaths before he could make the final turn.

"Are we here?" Sierra was reaching to unbuckle her seatbelt.

"It's just around the corner."

"So why did we stop?" Sierra's brow furrowed. "Are we going back home instead?"

Silas scanned the street, looking for inspiration. The Duncan house was a perfect excuse. "Do you see the house out your window?"

"Yeah." Sierra pressed her head against the window.

"Can you find anything special in their flowers?"

Sierra was quiet for a few moments while she stared out the window. Then she began to giggle.

"Why are there funny men in their yard?"

The sound of her laughter was a balm to Silas's heart. "Those are called garden gnomes. Which one is your favorite?"

Sierra pressed her forehead to the window again. This time, her head moved back and forth while she looked. "I like the yellow one."

"The one with the yellow hat or the one with the big sunflower in his hands?" Silas's nerves were almost calm.

"Both!" She giggled again. "The one with the hat has a big nose. Can I tell Grandma about him?"

Silas turned his head so he could see his daughter. "She would love that. Are you ready to see her?"

"Yes!" Sierra sat back in her seat with a giggle.

They drove around the final curve in the road, pulling up in front of a modest two-story house. A wave of memories slammed into Silas. He hadn't realized how homesick he had gotten.

The car was barely parked before the front door swung open and his parents stepped out. One look at his mom's face was all the confirmation he needed that they were in the right place. If there was an environment for Sierra to heal in, this was it.

Silas held Sierra's hand for comfort when they walked up the path towards his parents. She dropped it when they were close to the front door and ran into his mom's arms.

He looked at his dad, who had his arms stretched open wide.

"Welcome home, son. We're glad you're here."

* * *

SILAS DIDN'T THINK that being home would make a difference to Sierra, but after just two short days, she already had a little color in her cheeks. He sat on the back porch, watching her run around with her cousins, the laughter floating back to him a balm to his soul.

"Remind me why you are worried about her," his sister Rose said.

"You can't tell at the moment, but she's been in serious pain for several months now." Silas rubbed the back of his neck. "It's been awful."

"And the doctors don't know what is going on?" Rose had two daughters, Lacy and Chrissy. They were racing through the yard, their long brown hair trailing behind them while they chased Sierra. Being younger than Sierra didn't seem to matter to them. They knew she was a cousin and that was enough for them to take off running.

"We've seen specialists and done tests, but they don't have a diagnosis yet."

Rose rubbed Silas's arm. "I'm sorry. I know how hard that can be. Remember when Lacy was in the hospital?"

Silas nodded. Lacy went through a period of time where she had repeated seizures, and it took a while for the doctors to figure out what was happening. At the time, Rose called it her own personal torture chamber.

"Didn't it take them over an hour to find a vein for an I.V. one day?" Silas had offered to drive back from the city to help after that day, but Rose had stopped him.

"Yep. It was so hard to not be able to explain why the doctors were being mean to her."

Silas nodded. "At least Sierra understands what is going on. Her attitude is pretty amazing, considering that she's almost always in pain."

Rose leaned back against the chair. She looked nothing like Silas, having much lighter skin and light brown hair compared to his tan complexion and dark hair. People said they didn't look like siblings except for their deep brown eyes. Those were identical.

Silas appreciated having a sister he could talk to. "Do you know Sierra has started praying for me to find her a mom?"

"You're kidding, right?" Rose took a sip of her lemonade.

"I wish. I'm not sure what to do about it. We've talked about Zoe before. I thought Sierra understood why she didn't have a mom in her life, but now I'm not so sure."

"That's a hard one." Rose set her glass on the small table between them. "Have you thought about dating anyone?"

The vice that gripped Silas's chest at the thought of it was all the answer he needed. "It really just isn't the right time. I tried it a while back and gave up. I spend all day at work and then my life is consumed with taking care of Sierra in the evenings. It's too hard to fit dating into that schedule."

"Yeah. That's tricky. What about while you are here? We could watch Sierra while you go out."

Silas laughed. "Do you have some women lined up for

me? Last I checked, this town isn't exactly crawling with eligible bachelorettes who are lining up to date a single dad."

Rose winked at him. "I wouldn't be so sure about that."

Silas knew that look. Tension banded across his shoulders. "What did you do?"

His sister wasn't exactly subtle in the way she managed things. "I didn't officially *do* anything, yet. I just told a few of my friends that my handsome older brother was coming into town with his daughter and suggested that he might be looking for someone to hang out with."

"You're the worst. Besides, I'm not going to start a long-distance relationship. Once our visit is over, we'll be heading back to the city. That's a long drive for a simple movie night."

"Hear me out." Rose picked up her glass and began to stir the lemonade with her straw. "What if we have a barbeque in a couple of nights? We could all invite some friends over, and if someone happened to catch your eye, you could see where it goes. Maybe it would be good to go on a few dates, just as a trial run."

Silas took a cleansing breath. He folded his arms across his chest and watched his daughter running. Not dating had been an easy choice when Sierra was little. Now that she was beginning to think about a mom, did he owe it to her to try?

He uncrossed his arms and leaned forward in his chair to watch Sierra while she ran behind the playhouse. "I guess."

Rose let out a cheer. "For real?"

Silas nodded. "What harm could it do? It's not like I'm going to fall in love with anyone in the two weeks we're here."

"You never know."

Rose was clearly hoping for Silas to meet the love of his life, but he was pretty sure he already had. And he had blown it spectacularly. He had tried dating a few times over the years, but no one could measure up to the butterflies he had felt when he was around Hope. She had set a standard that was hard to beat.

Watching Sierra play, it was easy for Silas to let his guard down. "Hey sis, do you remember Hope Matthews?"

Rose turned to look at him, her eyebrows raised. "That's a name I haven't heard for years. Of course, I remember the girl you were head over heels in love with. Why do you ask?"

He hadn't been wanting to talk about Hope, but being at home was making him nostalgic. "I saw her the other day."

Rose was sitting forward now. "Oh really? Did you talk to her?"

"Nope." Silas turned his face forward to watch Sierra, so he didn't have to see his sister's disapproving expression.

She nudged him with her elbow. "Spill. I want details. How did she look?"

Silas regretted opening his mouth. "She's just as beautiful as she was the day I left, although she looked like she was in a lot of pain."

"I'm confused."

"I was at the doctor's office with Sierra, and Hope was there getting x-rays." He followed Sierra with his eyes again, smiling when she ducked behind a tree to pop out and scare Chrissy.

"Do you wish you talked to her? You could have gotten her number."

Silas shook his head. "I'm pretty sure I still have it, but I don't think she'd want me to interrupt her life. She looked pretty happy."

"Was she with someone?" Rose was leaning forward, hanging on to every word.

"She was definitely there with a guy. It happened so fast, I didn't look for rings." Silas thought about the way the guy helped her walk to the car. The love on his face was evident. "They were pretty chummy though."

"I'm sorry, Silas. Why are you asking about her?"

Silas reached for a square patio pillow, turning it over in his hands while he thought. "I blame you and all your talk about dating. Seeing her stirred up memories that I had buried a long time ago. I can't help but think about her now that I'm home."

Rose reached out to rest her hand on his leg. "I know you didn't want to leave her. Did you ever tell her why?"

The memory of leaving Hope was one Silas could never forget. "I didn't have the chance. Besides, I knew how Hope felt about intimacy and marriage. She wasn't going to understand that I had slept with Zoe. Not when she was saving herself for marriage."

"I thought you wrote her a note."

Silas shook his head. "I couldn't find the words."

"So, you left her with no excuse at all?" Her mouth gaped open. "That's awful."

"I told her I'd see her at the prom. I figured we could have a last dance and then I'd leave. Zoe threw a fit about that." He blinked against the tears that pricked the corners of his eyes. "I left my heart behind when I followed Zoe. I didn't deserve to get it back."

"And then Sierra was born."

"Exactly. She healed me in ways I didn't expect. What happens if I can't find a way to heal her, too?" Silas was putting words to the fears he had.

Rose swiveled her chair so she was facing Silas. "You are going to find an answer. I know it. Sierra is so lucky to have a dad like you."

"Thanks." Silas looked up to see Sierra tripping in the grass, taking Chrissy down with her. They both began to cry.

"And that's our cue." Rose jumped to her feet, running to her daughter while Silas ran to his.

An assessment of the girls showed that no one was too banged up. Sierra had a small grass stain on her knee, but her hands were fine. Chrissy had a shallow scrape on her palm where she fell on a stick.

"How about we head inside and see if Grandma has any ice cream?" Silas asked. That was the best cure for tears.

The three girls cheered.

Once they were settled down at the kitchen table, Rose

reached for Silas's arm. "We got interrupted out there, but I want you to know how much I admire you. You've been the best dad to Sierra. I'm glad you guys came here so we can get to know her better. It's good for the girls to have cousins."

"Thanks, Rose." Silas took a sip of lemonade and let his mind wander back to Hope. Her ranch was just a fifteen-minute drive away from his parent's house. He was glad she wasn't around to tempt him.

By the time the ice cream was gone, all the tears had dried up. The girls ran back outside to play, and Silas pulled out his laptop.

"Are you okay keeping an eye on them while I check in with work?"

Rose nodded. "Of course." She headed towards the back porch and Silas turned his focus to the screen. He had gotten behind in his work assignments, and although his team was trying to be patient, Silas didn't want to keep them waiting. He flipped to the first screen and began to read the report.

An hour later the girls came barging through the door. Lacy and Chrissy were laughing loudly, poking each other back and forth, but Sierra was more subdued. Silas recognized that look. Sierra took her cup of water from Rose but barely drank a sip.

That was Silas's warning that work was done for the day. He held his arms out, lifting Sierra onto his lap when she came near. "Are they tummy goblins acting up again?"

Sierra's eyes welled with tears. "I just want to play with my cousins."

Her tears tore his heart in half. "You guys have been playing outside for a long time. What if we watch a movie now? Aunt Rose will get some popcorn ready, and I'll get the pillows."

He glanced at Rose over the top of Sierra's head, hoping she'd understand. The concern on her face vanished when she grinned at the girls. "That sounds like a great idea. Lacy and Chrissy, why don't you go help Uncle Silas and Sierra to figure out what you guys want to watch. I'll be there once the popcorn is ready."

Silas felt a surge of gratitude that flowed through his body. Instead of having to take care of Sierra on his own, he had help. He had been doing everything on his own for so long, he had forgotten how good it felt to be part of a team.

"Thank you," he mouthed. Then he led the girls into the family room and got them tucked in with blankets and pillows. If things went as he expected, Sierra would be asleep in minutes.

Silas sat on one side of the couch and Rose sat on the other, their girls between them. A few minutes later, their mom walked into the room.

"Any room for Grandma?" She nestled in between Sierra and Chrissy, smiling as her granddaughters leaned against her sides.

Silas leaned back and tried to follow the story of the

talking bear and his penguin friend, but soon his eyelids were drooping as well. For the first time in a long time, he was able to completely relax. He allowed his eyes to close and drifted off to sleep, for once not worrying about Sierra. With his family watching, he knew she was in good hands.

CHAPTER 5

Hope was standing in the middle of the pig barn, staring down at a heavy bag of pig feed while she groaned in frustration. She had every reason to stay away from the ranch work, but she had missed helping. Picking up an entire feed bag with only one good arm was definitely out of the question, but feeding the pigs one scoop of food at a time wasn't proving to be as effective as she'd hoped.

She was kicking the rungs of the pigsty when Monroe found her. He laughed when he saw the open food bag beside her.

"Need a hand?" Monroe reached for the scoop, gently prying it out of her hand. He looked different than usual, but it took a moment for Hope to pinpoint why. Then she realized that for the first time since meeting him, Monroe's face was completely relaxed. He wasn't clenching his jaw like he usually did when he was stressed.

Hope leaned against the fence, kicking against it with the heel of her boot. "I thought I'd help Thomas with the pigs, but my broken arm isn't cooperating."

"What are you trying to do?" Monroe grabbed the feed bag. "I'm guessing it has something to do with this bag?"

She held back a grimace. "Yes. I was trying to dump it down the chute, but it takes forever if you have to scoop it out."

"Got it." Monroe hefted the bag, angling the opening towards the chute.

Hope felt a mixture of frustration and gratitude as the food rattled to the bottom. She placed her hand on Monroe's shoulder. "Thanks. I didn't bring you here so you'd have to help with farm work."

He nodded. "I know, but it's actually kind of fun. What else would you be doing if you weren't hurt?"

"Riding my horses. I miss them."

Monroe folded the now empty bag and placed it in the trash can. "Would you believe I've never ridden a horse before."

Hope shook her head. "Seriously?" She waved her cast in the air. "You only have one day left and I can't even take you riding. You're just going to have to come back soon."

"I can't believe you're staying here for the rest of the month."

It was going to be the longest Hope had ever gone without seeing her best friend in years. "I know. I'm going to miss you."

"Me too." Monroe flicked one of the braids Bree had

done for Hope that morning. "Since we only have a day left, what else do you want to show me in this small town of yours?"

Hope hooked her arm in Monroe's and pulled him towards the chicken coop. "We have Bree's graduation this afternoon. There's going to be some great people watching opportunities there. And then I think we're going to a barbecue with some of Bree's friends."

"It sounds like a full day."

They were standing in front of the coop. Hope unlatched the door and grabbed a basket. "Ready to gather eggs like a real rancher?"

"Bring it."

Hope laughed as Monroe gingerly tried to slide his hand under the first hen only to jerk it back when the chicken pecked his hand. "Um, do they all do that?"

"There's lots of nests that aren't being protected right now. Do you want to start with them?"

Monroe nodded. Hope loved watching his face light up as the basket filled with a dozen eggs. "Do you guys actually eat this many eggs? I imagine you're overloaded by the end of the week."

Hope handed the basket to Monroe and then slipped her hand under the brooding hen, retrieving a few more eggs. "My mom is pretty amazing at getting through them. Between the cooking and baking she does, it's a wonder she doesn't need more than we usually get."

After a quick trip to the kitchen to drop off the basket, Hope was off again, leading Monroe to the pasture where the horses were grazing. "Aren't they pretty?" She tilted forward to rest her arm on one of the fence posts, trying to ignore the hard cast that was getting in her way.

"I knew you came from a ranching family, but I don't think I ever gave much thought to how it would feel being stuck in the city. Was it hard to leave this behind?"

Hope watched the horses as they dipped their heads to the ground. "Yes and no. I love the open land, and I miss my animals, but I don't miss the hard parts of the ranch. It would be one thing if the weather always cooperated and the animals never got sick, but those are just some of the difficulties of running a large ranch. It can be exhausting."

She had seen more than her fair share of ranch emergencies. It felt like something was always either falling apart or on the brink of it. Hope hadn't realized how run down she was until she left for college. Once her classes began, her energy shifted into a mental workout. She didn't miss the physical labor on the ranch at all.

Monroe watched the horses, his brow furrowed. "So, it's easier to sing about country life than it is to actually live it?"

"Much." Hope thought back to the weeks before she left the ranch. Silas had left her a few months before she headed to school, but her heart was still tender enough that she could put that ache and longing into her songs. "I can sing about being a cowgirl all day long, but I honestly didn't realize how much living with my boots in the dirt grounds me."

"Don't tell me you're going to fall in love with the land

all over again and leave me behind." Monroe had a teasing glint in his eye, but Hope understood the seriousness behind his words.

"I'm still planning to come back at the end of the month. If I want to have a real go at my music, I need to be where the talent scouts are. I can't exactly audition for much from here."

"Just promise me you won't get swept off your feet by some handsome guy here in town and decide to put your roots down."

Hope's mind flashed to seeing Silas. He had definitely been someone she'd consider putting roots down with, but he was nothing more than a high school fling. "I don't think you have anything to worry about. For all I know, you're going to catch the eye of some beautiful cowgirl tonight and she's going to sweep you off your feet. I'll go off on tour somewhere and come back to find you wearing cowboy boots and a hat."

Monroe threw his head back and laughed. "Can you imagine me in boots? I don't think they're my style."

"Then it's a good thing I'm the one singing the country songs. Let's get back to the house so we can eat before the graduation festivities."

They walked back to a house filled with lively conversations. Porter and Emily were sitting in the family room, and Hope remembered that they had news to share. She tried to glance at Emily's stomach to see if there was a baby bump, but she didn't want to stare. The couple would share the news when they were ready.

Thomas sat in an armchair, and Hazel sat on his lap. Hope loved seeing how happy each of her brothers were. She wandered into the kitchen, where Reid and Millie were helping Mom Matthews to stack cookies on a giant platter.

"Are you planning to feed the entire neighborhood?" Hope asked.

Mom Matthews shook her head. "Maybe. I'm not sure how many people are going to this party, but I've never heard anyone complain about too many cookies."

"She's right about that," Millie said. She glanced at her phone and then grabbed a cookie. "We'd better get going."

"I thought graduation didn't start for a couple more hours," Monroe said.

"I'm a teacher, so I'll be sitting on the stage with all the other staff. I'm also helping the kids to line up so the ceremony goes well."

Reid grabbed his own cookie and handed another one over to Millie. "Let's go."

Hope watched them walk off and her heart soared. The beginnings of a song stirred in her mind. Somehow, against seemingly impossible odds, the Matthews family men were finding love. She had begun to wonder if she was going to be the first of the siblings to get married.

Instead, she was gladly single and following her dreams. Hope lifted her phone and glanced at the screen. She was waiting to see if she'd gotten invited to travel with The Ginny Brooks band, but each day that passed left her feeling more certain that they had moved on. She couldn't exactly blame them. A performer who fell on her face wasn't exactly the best opening act to hire.

Monroe saw her reach for her phone. He rubbed her shoulder. "They haven't chosen anyone yet, which means you still have a chance."

Bree walked in right when Monroe was speaking. "What do you have a chance for?"

"I auditioned to open for a famous act, but I don't think they are going to call."

"Who is it?" Bree was tilting up on her toes.

"I'm not allowed to say, but you'll be the first person I tell." Hope slid her phone into her pocket. The news wasn't going to come any faster if she was staring at the screen.

"I came downstairs to find you." Bree held a small bag up. "Will you do my makeup for graduation? You can do that with one hand, right?"

Hope shoved a piece of cookie into her mouth, chewing quickly. "Of course. Do you want something fancy or something more casual?" She followed behind her sister to the bathroom where Bree began opening drawers.

"How about something in the middle. Smoky eyes and a touch of lipstick?"

"Good call." Hope spilled the makeup bag onto the counter so she could rifle through the various colors of eyeshadow.

"How do you feel?" Hope asked.

Bree clasped her hands in front of her. "Is it strange to say I'm feeling a little bit of probably every emotion out there? I'm excited, of course, but I'm also sad to be leaving my friends behind. I'm eager to see what the future holds but terrified I'll mess it up somehow. I'm glad I'll never have to go to another high school math class until I realize that now my classes are going to be college level. Like I said, it's a bit of everything."

Hope gave her sister a hug from behind, resting her cheek against Bree's hair. "I'm so proud of you. It takes a lot to be able to graduate with high honors. I think you're going to do great in college."

"What if I fail?"

The question was one that Hope had fought with over and over again in her pursuit of music. "If you fail, you're going to get back up, dust yourself off, and then call your big sister. I'll be standing by with a big box of Band-Aids to patch you up and send you on your way again."

Bree giggled. "I'm not a five-year-old girl who fell off her horse for the first time."

"I know, but sometimes it will feel like you are. You're going to make mistakes, because that is what humans do. But honestly, Bree. I can't wait to see where the world takes you."

THREE HOURS later Bree was walking across the stage to cheers and applause from her family. She waved at them when she sat back down, holding her diploma in the air.

Hope's heart swelled with pride. She had been proudly watching Bree grow up since the day she was born. If ever there was a firecracker who was going to take the world by storm, it was Bree.

After a final round of photos, the family headed towards their cars. Hope and Monroe climbed in the back seat, letting Bree have shotgun. Mom Matthews was driving towards the barbeque when Hope's stomach began to churn. She recognized the route her mom was taking.

Sure enough, before long the road opened onto a long street. Hope began counting the houses as they drove. There wasn't any logical reason why they'd be heading to the Foster house, but that was the direction they seemed to be going.

Hope cleared her throat. "Uh, I forgot to ask. Where is the barbeque tonight?"

Bree turned around to face her. "My friend Mia is having a party. She graduated this year, too."

"That's fun." There must have been something in Hope's expression because her mom glanced at her in the rear-view mirror, her mouth turning into a small circle of understanding.

"I'm sorry, Hope. I thought you knew where we were going." Mom slowed the car. "Do you want me to take you home first?"

Hope closed her eyes and took a steadying breath. There was no reason why she couldn't go to Silas's house. He was safely tucked away in the city. All she would have to deal with were some uncomfortable memories.

"What is going on?" Bree looked anxiously from her mom to Hope. "Is there something I should know?"

Monroe was tense in the seat beside her. Hope had seconds to pull herself together before she ruined Bree's happy mood.

"I'm good. I just wanted to make sure the crowd wasn't too big. It's still a little painful if someone jostles my arm." It was only part of a lie. Hope did have to be careful with her cast, but she was more worried about protecting her heart.

Mom Matthews studied her face, and then gave an almost imperceptible nod. She drove the rest of the way to the Foster house while Hope tried to blink back tears. This was Bree's special graduation day. If she wanted to celebrate with friends, Hope was going to stand by her side and be supportive no matter the cost.

There was just the pesky matter of the tears that continued to well up in her eyes when they pulled in front of the house. Hope "accidentally" banged her knee on her way out of the car so she had an excuse for her red eyes.

"Are you okay?" Bree asked.

Hope sniffled and wiped her face. "I'm good. Why don't you and mom go in? Monroe and I will be there in a minute once I look like I haven't just been crying."

Bree nodded and headed for the door, none the wiser. Mom Matthews wrapped her arms around Hope's shoulders. "I'm sorry, sweetheart. I didn't even make the connection."

By this point, Monroe was glancing back and forth between mother and daughter. He reached for Hope's hand. "What is going on? Do I need to take you somewhere else?"

Hope shook her head. "Do you remember the guy who abandoned me my senior year?"

"Yeah."

"The party is at his house. He doesn't live here anymore, so it isn't really a big deal. It just caught me by surprise." Hope was hoping if she said it didn't matter enough times, she'd start to believe the words.

"Do you want to take a minute to compose yourself?" Her mom reached into her purse and pulled out a tissue. "I can tell Linda you're bringing the cookies in, so it doesn't feel awkward."

"Yes, please." Hope leaned back against Monroe's chest, trying to breathe deeply.

He wrapped his arm around her shoulder, waiting to speak until her mom disappeared through the side gate. "What can I do?"

Hope covered her face with her good hand. "High school happened so long ago, I shouldn't still be hung up on him. I guess I'm having a hard time letting this one go."

"What was his name again?" Monroe was a steadying presence against her back.

"Silas."

"That's right." He rubbed her shoulder. "Do you want to talk about it?"

Hope gave a small shrug. "There's not much to say. I was young. I loved him and I thought he loved me too." She dabbed at her eyes. "At the time I thought we were going to be one of those couples that made it all the way. I can't remember the percentage of people who dated in high school that actually stay married, but I knew we'd beat that statistic."

"And then he broke up with you?"

The tears were coming harder. Hope blinked furiously, trying to stop them. "That's just it. He didn't break up with me."

"So, you broke up with him." It was a statement, not a question. Monroe was trying to follow along, but Hope knew she wasn't explaining herself well.

"Nope. We didn't break up at all. One minute we were making plans for prom. The next, he dropped off the face of the earth with no explanation." The shock of being stood up still stung. Hope pressed her lips together, trying to tamp down her pain.

"Oh, Sunshine. I'm so sorry." Monroe pulled her into a hug, and Hope allowed herself a few minutes to mourn for the loss that was resurfacing.

"If I ever meet the guy, want me to beat him up?"

He was ridiculous, but the offer made Hope smile. "How about instead of beating him up, we just plan to never see him?" She didn't mention seeing Silas at the urgent care clinic. It would make him upset and there was nothing he could do about it.

"Sounds good to me. Are you ready?"

Hope dabbed at her eyes one final time. They would be a little puffy, but no one would be looking at her too closely. "Let's grab those cookies."

She headed towards the house with Monroe close behind. Bringing her best friend home was turning out to be more of a help than she imagined. He was her rock.

The side gate was clearly marked as the entrance, which made Hope happy. She didn't want to walk through the house, where there were pictures of the family lining the walls. Her heart was feeling bruised enough without seeing visual reminders of Silas everywhere she looked.

Hope set the platter of cookies on a table, where it was immediately surrounded by a group of teenage girls with Bree leading the pack.

"I told you, my mom makes the best cookies." She grabbed two cookies and led her friends off to another part of the yard where a group of boys were gathering.

It was time to face the most uncomfortable part of the afternoon. Hope made her way over to where Mrs. Foster stood talking with her mom. She had gotten to know Silas's mom fairly well in high school. At one point, she thought she would be her future mother-in-law. Now the woman standing in front of her was someone who had no idea the pain Hope had been through.

Mrs. Foster turned to greet Hope. As they exchanged pleasantries, her face lit up. "I'm so glad you're here. I'm sure Silas will want to say hi."

She kept talking but the words were muffled. Hope leaned against Monroe for support.

"He's here?" Her heart began to beat so quickly, the blood was rushing to her head.

Mrs. Foster nodded. "He just ran inside for some ice. Here he comes now."

Hope was watching in slow motion as Mrs. Foster turned and began to wave her hand in the air. "Silas. Over here. Come say hello to an old friend."

CHAPTER 6

Silas dumped a bag of ice into the cooler filled with cans of soda. He glanced over at his mom who stood with a tall man. He didn't recognize the wavy brown hair, but if it was an old friend, the guy could be anyone. It was probably someone from the football team.

Sierra was standing on her tiptoes, reaching for the tray of cookies that had appeared while he was inside. "Just one cookie, Pumpkin," he said. "I don't want the tummy goblins to come while our friends are here."

Her lips turned down into a pout. "But dad, I want one of each kind."

Silas reached for her hand. "How about one cookie now and one after you eat some carrot sticks?"

Those were the magic words Sierra was waiting for. She grinned and dropped his hand, running to the veggie tray.

Silas headed towards his mom. He was almost to her

side when the man turned. The profile of his face looked vaguely familiar, but Silas couldn't place him. The man stepped to the side and Silas froze in place.

It wasn't the man his mom was calling him over to greet. It was Hope. Somehow, instead of being back in the city, she was standing in his backyard.

Silas wanted to head back to the house, but it was too late.

"Here he is." His mom was beaming with a smile that felt a little too forced. "Silas, you remember Hope, right? She was just telling me about how she broke her arm."

A sharp pain lanced straight to Silas's heart when he took the final steps to stand by his mother's side. She was acting like Hope and Silas were just old high school pals. It didn't make sense that his mom would forget that they had dated in the past. Looking back and forth between Hope and his mom, Silas realized why.

When Silas left to follow Zoe, he hadn't given his parents an explanation. They didn't know that he had shattered Hope's world when he left without a word. They also weren't around to see the nights he sat on his bed, staring at a wall, trying not to break down and cry.

To his mom, Hope was just another high school crush. Not the girl he had deeply loved and then abandoned.

Hope met his eyes, her expression mirroring the torture he felt. Every moment with Hope crashed into his mind at once. He had to look away. There were too many memories wrapped up in that look, and Silas couldn't stomach them. Especially not with her boyfriend standing protectively at Hope's back.

It didn't take long to recognize where he had seen the man. This was the guy who was with Hope at the doctor's office.

Silas glanced at Hope's hand where she was grasping her phone. No ring. She probably wasn't married, but he had seen enough to know that she was in a close relationship with the man behind her. It was probably only a matter of time before he proposed.

Remembering basic manners was a task that Silas's brain struggled to do, but he stretched his hand out to Hope's friend. "Hi. I'm Silas. And you are?"

"Monroe."

Monroe's grip was firm, his hand squeezing with just enough force to let Silas know that he knew who Silas was, and he wasn't pleased to see him. Why would he be? There was no reason to believe that Hope would hide a past relationship.

Turning to face her was impossible, but Silas did, holding his hand awkwardly out before dropping it to his side. Shaking hands with her felt like an insult.

"Hi, Hope." Silas's mouth was dry. He scanned the yard for Sierra, wanting to look anywhere except into the deep, gray eyes that sent his pulse ricocheting through his body. He didn't realize how quickly the memories would come flooding back, but seeing Hope standing in front of him was making it impossible to forget how much he had loved holding her in his arms.

She leaned back against Monroe, and he wrapped his hand around her waist in a familiar way, tearing a gash through Silas's heart. He was the one who was supposed to be holding her like that, but he had lost that chance seven years before.

"Hello." Hope's voice sent a wave of remembrance through Silas that threatened to knock him off his feet. There was a time he would have gone to the ends of the earth just to hear that voice. Now, each syllable sent a shock wave through his body.

Silas scanned the yard looking for any excuse to get away from this personal torture chamber.

"Did you know Hope was auditioning to open for a big country singer?" His mom was talking, but Silas's head was underwater, waves of regret rolling over him so fast, he could barely breathe.

He was desperate now, praying for a reason to leave the conversation. The Lord had punished him enough for his indiscretions when he was in high school. He had given him a daughter, but she had come at a steep, steep price. There was no reason to believe God cared enough about him to save him from every awkward conversation.

Still, somewhere in the heavens, God must have been listening because a sharp cry rose above the din of the crowded yard.

"Daddy?"

Sierra's panicked voice sent Silas spinning on his heels. "It was good to see you," he said, before running across the yard to the house.

Sierra stood in the doorway, her face pale.

"What's wrong, Pumpkin?" Silas scooped her up into his arms, holding her tightly against his chest.

"I couldn't find you. Lacy said I couldn't play with her dolls, and Chrissy stuck her tongue out at me."

There was no emergency, except for a small squabble between cousins. That was something Silas could handle on his own. He set Sierra down and led her into the house, grateful for the chance to get away from the yard. Maybe God was listening after all.

Hours later, Silas found himself alone in the kitchen, up to his elbows in bubbles as he scrubbed down the last of the dishes. A lone platter remained on the counter with an intricate flower design that circled the edge. Silas didn't usually pay attention to what dishes looked like, but this platter was the exception. He'd be able to pick it out of a lineup.

The thought of putting dishes into a lineup made him smile, but it quickly fell. There was a reason the platter was so familiar. He had eaten more cookies off of it than he could count as a teenager. A wave of nostalgia hit Silas, and he sank into a chair, burying his face in his hands.

Why was Hope here? She was supposed to be in the city, following her dreams. Not back in the country, stirring up feelings that he had long since buried. He figured most people felt a little twinge when they ran into an ex, but Hope sent his emotions flying.

The problem was that he had never gotten any closure with her. He recognized how cowardly it was to walk away from the relationship, but he had been young. He hadn't known what to do. Somehow, he hoped walking away would sever his feelings.

Now, seeing her with the man by her side, he knew those feelings had been lying dormant, simmering beneath the surface. All it took was a whiff of her perfume and he was flooded with memories. The feel of her soft skin beneath his hands when he draped his hand across her shoulder. The way her lips curled into a smile before pressing against his. The sound of her laughter when he told a corny joke, ringing out so loudly that heads would turn.

Hope was everything Silas wanted in a woman, but one very large mistake had been all it took for him to run without looking back. He had been too young and too foolish to keep holding on. He was shaking his head back and forth when his mom came into the room.

She walked to his side and gave him a quick hug. "Thanks for doing the dishes."

"No problem." Silas rubbed his face a few times to hide any trace of emotion. He wasn't about to tell his mom how he felt about Hope. She would make a fuss, and the day had already been long enough.

Mom Foster walked to the counter where the platter sat and held it up with a sigh. "I forgot to send this home with

Bree. I'll have to run it over there next time I'm out. Hopefully they don't need it for any of their own graduation celebrations."

"I can take it." The words were tumbling out of Silas's mouth before his brain had time to catch up with what his heart was saying. He opened his mouth to take the words back, but his mom was already turning, a look of relief painted across her face.

"That would be amazing." She glanced at the clock. "Would you mind taking it over now? Before it gets buried under other things?"

A giant cow patty had dropped in front of Silas, and he had stepped right into it. He scrambled for an excuse. "What about Sierra? It's almost her bedtime."

Mom Foster shook her head. "Remember the slumber party we promised the girls? Mia is painting their nails right now. I don't think they'll be falling asleep any time soon."

Silas was caught. If he protested further, his mom would be suspicious that something was up. "Alright then. I'll head there now."

He picked up the platter and headed to the family room where he found Sierra giggling with her aunts.

"Hey, Pumpkin. I'm going to run a little errand. Are you okay here with Aunt Rose and Aunt Mia?"

She glanced up, and the grin that spread across her face unraveled one of the knots in his stomach. Anyone could see how happy she was here. He should have come much sooner.

"We're doing nails." Sierra kissed his cheek and turned her attention back to her manicure. She glanced back at him. "I love you, Daddy."

"I love you, too, Pumpkin."

There was nothing else stopping Silas from leaving. He lingered in the doorway for a moment, taking in the sight of his daughter. She was the reason Silas had left Hope behind, and he would never feel sorry for that.

The sun painted streaks of gold across the sky while crickets chirped so loudly, Silas could hear them through his closed windows as he drove. With aching tenderness in his heart, he started the drive up Old Ranch Road. The road was familiar, from the uneven juts in the pavement to the curve that swung to the right before he turned into the driveway.

How many times had he driven Hope home, only to stay in the car, parked in front of her house, while they talked for hours? He tried to push the memories out of his mind. That was a long time ago, and they had both moved on.

Heat enveloped his body when he climbed out of his car, standing in front of the Matthews Ranch. A cool breeze would pick up once the sun fully set, but for now, the warmth was comforting.

Not much had changed about the house. It could use another paint job, but the porch looked the same. Another pang shot through Silas. He had first told Hope he loved her while standing on those steps.

Silas grunted and reached for the platter. The sooner he

could drop it off, the sooner he could get on his way back home. He was keeping his composure until he came to the first step and stopped. Almost without thinking, he gripped the rail and then slid his hand to the underside, sliding his fingers back and forth.

Coarse scratches in the wood met his fingers. Only two people in the world knew why the wood was rough and what it meant.

H + S. Hope had pulled out a pocket knife and scratched their initials into the gap between the rungs, giggling while she did so. "My mom would kill me if she knew what I was doing, but she'll never find out."

It became a habit to touch the engraved letters every time Silas dropped her off. Now, his fingers slid there of their own accord. Some habits were hard to break.

Silas wrenched his hand away and walked up the rest of the steps with a firm grip on the platter. He only hesitated for a moment before ringing the doorbell. Just long enough to smooth his features so he looked like nothing more than a casual friend dropping by with a forgotten item. All the while, he silently prayed that no one would be home.

Given the number of cars in the driveway, there was little chance of that happening. One car stood out from the others, the bright red paint sticking out like a sore thumb compared to the ranch vehicles. Silas guessed that it was Monroe's car. The guy clearly didn't belong in the country, so why was he here?

A swell of laughter reached Silas's ears before it

abruptly stopped. Moments later, the door was flung open by Bree.

"Silas!" She reached for the platter, setting it on a small entryway table. "My mom was just teasing me for forgetting this."

Silas could feel his heart slowing. Bree was probably the best person to answer the door if anyone had to answer at all. She was too wrapped up in the excitement of her graduation to care that he was there.

"Congrats on today," he said. He turned to leave but knew he had something more he had to say. Gulping once, he cleared his throat as he turned back to face Bree. "Is, uh, Hope around?"

Bree's expression wasn't difficult to read. The surprise that flickered across her face softened to a resigned smile. Clearly, Bree knew who he was. He had spent hours of his time hanging out on the Matthews Ranch while he and Hope dated. He could only imagine the stories Bree had heard when he left her sister behind without an explanation.

That was why, against his better judgment, he was standing on the porch. Hope deserved to know why he left, even if it was seven years too late and she had more than moved on.

Bree reached for his arm, giving it a small pat. "It will be good for you two to talk."

With that, she bounded into the house, leaving Silas empty-handed on the doorstep, his stomach swirling with doubt.

He craned his neck around, wondering how rude it would be to leave instead of waiting around. The only thing between him and his escape was an eighteen-year-old girl who probably wouldn't care if he vanished. But Hope would. He wouldn't do that to her again.

A warm breeze tickled his cheek and he inhaled deeply, letting his lungs fill until they were bursting before he held his breath. After a count to three, he let the air slowly release. He had learned to calm his breathing when he was at the doctor's office with Sierra, listening to yet another round of bad news. He could do the same here.

It didn't matter how much he pined for Hope. Based on the things he had seen, she was doing great without him. Time had allowed her to move on and he really needed to do the same.

Silas stood straighter. He wasn't a young man anymore. He had a successful job and a beautiful daughter. It was time to stop whining about past would haves and could haves and let them sink back into his memories. The sooner he was away from this place, the easier that would be.

Bree was shouting somewhere deep in the house. Silas shut the door so bugs wouldn't get in. Then he walked over to the railing and leaned against it. He could be patient, even though his heart raced a million miles an hour.

He was crossing one foot over the other when the door swung open. Silas straightened up. He was expecting Hope, but he hadn't expected to see her face, mid-laugh as she opened the door. She jumped when she saw him, and her face quickly fell. Clearly Bree hadn't told her sister who was there.

"Silas." His name fell from her lips in a whisper, the way it always had when love and longing filled those two syllables. She pressed her hands to her side and said his name again, this time with a coldness behind the words. "Silas. What are you doing here?"

The words were stripped of emotion. Hope was speaking to him much like you'd speak to the cashier at a grocery store. He was a random person standing on her doorstep and nothing more.

Silas wanted to spring forward and wrap his arm around her. He ached to know everything about her, including what happened to her arm. He wanted to know how Monroe fit into her life. Was she happy?

Instead, he straightened his shoulders and looked her straight in the eye. "I was hoping we could talk."

A heaviness filled the air, making it difficult for Silas to breathe. There was so much he wanted to say, and yet he wasn't sure he'd be able to get the words out. He needed a chance to explain.

Pain flickered across Hope's face, and she closed her eyes, the rise and fall of her chest the only indicator that she was trying to steady her breathing much like he was. She glanced into the house. Was she looking for Monroe to come save her?

Then, with a small sigh, she stepped onto the porch, letting the door swing shut behind her.

CHAPTER 7

Hope wished her professors were watching her now, because she was sure that she hadn't let a flicker of pain cross her face. She had learned how to tune out everything else, including her emotions, before every performance. Now, standing on the porch with Silas, she schooled her face so he couldn't see her racing thoughts while she watched him stand in the exact spot where they had shared their first kiss.

When he first left, she told herself he was just a high school crush. She tried to convince herself that she wanted to go to college without him and follow her love of singing. It made it easier than thinking about the relationship she hoped would last through the years.

"It was mutual," she had lied, telling her friends she didn't care that he was gone. She'd wear a smile all day and then burst into tears the second she got into her car. He hadn't just broken her heart. He had taken it with him, with no explanation, and left her with a hollow in her chest that took months to fill.

Every relationship had been tainted by Silas. She knew how incredibly deeply she had fallen in love, and she also knew how quickly that could end. It was impossible to give her heart fully to someone when she kept waiting for them to throw it back in her face.

Silas was looking at her now with eyes that were so familiar, and yet so different. This was her Silas. The years dropped away, and she was transported back to her high school days. She ached to step into his arms, just to see if she still fit.

It was time to take control of the situation. "I'm not sure I have anything to say to you."

The words were harsh, but true. She watched him flinch back as if struck. It should feel good to finally speak her mind, but all Hope saw was the pain in his eyes.

"That's okay. I think I have enough words for the both of us." Silas gripped the railing with one hand, the veins in his hand tracing dark lines across his skin. He was paler than she remembered. The Silas from her past had been tanned from all the time they spent running around the ranch.

Hope recognized the pleading in his voice. She may not owe him anything, but she had been working on having grace for the people who upset her. They were all God's children. Even Silas, who she had secretly wished would end up somewhere with pitchforks and flames.

"You've got five minutes. Talk fast."

He flinched again, tightening his grip on the rail. Then he began to speak.

"Look. I know you don't owe me anything, let alone some of your time. I did a lot of things in high school that I'm not proud of, but ditching you was one of the worst. You didn't deserve that."

Hope's lips pressed tightly together. He was telling her things she already knew. "You're right."

Silas tapped the rail. "I know you've got a new life and I'm sure you don't think about our days together. I never thought I'd see you again, much less be able to talk to you, but for some reason we keep crossing paths. I wanted to tell you why I left."

He was saying words she had ached to hear seven years ago. Now, she had closed that part of her heart. The man standing before her was even more handsome than he had been in high school. But that was all he was. A pretty face.

Hope didn't need pretty. And she didn't need his explanations. She had moved on.

She cleared her throat, willing her voice to be steady. "What if I don't want your explanations?"

The words hit their mark. Silas blinked slowly, not understanding what she was saying. "You don't want to know?"

Hope shook her head. "It doesn't take a genius to figure things out. We graduated seven years ago, and you're back here with a daughter who looks like she's ready for kindergarten. Whatever our relationship was, you seemed to move on pretty quickly. Simply put, I was more in love with you than you were with me. And that's okay. People fall out of love. I've moved on."

There was a slight quiver in her voice, but Hope was keeping the tears at bay. She had maybe another minute before they'd begin to fall. Hope had already cried far too many tears to count over Silas. She wasn't going to give him the satisfaction of watching her cry now.

"If there's nothing else, I've really got to go."

Hope turned towards the door. She was reaching for the knob when Silas cleared his throat. "Her name is Sierra, and she was born four months after we graduated."

A chill raced down Hope's spine as she slowly turned.

Silas bowed his head. "You know I dated Zoe before you. I . . ." He trailed off, but Hope could put the pieces together.

"You got her pregnant."

There had been hushed rumors, of course. Zoe had denied being pregnant until she couldn't hide the baby bump anymore. Now Hope was supposed to believe that Silas was the father, and he hadn't known? There was no way.

Fire raced through her veins, the anger coming in red hot. "So, I guess all those times you whispered to me in school about being excited for our future were a lie. You couldn't have been wanting to be faithful to me when you had already gotten someone pregnant."

Betrayal stung her heart and her words tumbled out faster than before. "How could you have held onto that lie? Were you ever going to tell me?"

She could feel the flush rising in her cheeks. Hope had boundaries firmly set when it came to intimacy. She was saving herself for marriage, but she knew Silas hadn't felt the same way. He had agreed to respect her boundaries when they were dating. She was so in love with him, she hadn't cared what he had done in his previous relationships.

Silas held his hands out, pleading with her. "I slept with Zoe one time, and we broke up shortly afterwards. I'd say it was a mistake, but I got my daughter out of that night. I'll never say she's a mistake."

The sincerity in his eyes was genuine, but Hope was done listening to him. How could he hide something like that from her? She clenched her fists, wishing she could punch Silas in the face. She could have saved herself years of heartache if he had just been honest.

"Well, I'm glad that worked out for you." Hope rubbed a hand across her face. Seeing Silas again had dredged up memories from the past, but talking to him was throwing salt into aching wounds.

"Hope, what was I supposed to do?" His voice was quiet, almost pleading.

A million answers flew through Hope's mind, but there was only one she cared about. "You could have told me. Do you remember when the rumors began about Zoe being pregnant? I asked you, straight up, if there was any way you could be the father. I knew you didn't have the same standards as I did when it came to relationships, but I never thought you would lie to my face."

"I didn't know I was the father. She didn't tell me until the week before prom."

"So, you left with her." Hope slumped against the front door, the fight in her gone. "You left without saying goodbye."

Now Silas was the one with fire in his eyes. "She made me promise not to say a word. I had to choose her if I ever wanted to see the baby." His face darkened. "I had broken up with Zoe because we didn't see eye to eye on very many things. I had no idea how manipulative she could be. When she held the birth of our child over me, I followed her out of town and never looked back. I'm not sure what I could have done differently, but in the end, I'd make that choice again and again if it meant I could be Sierra's dad."

He fell so silent, Hope could feel her heart pounding in her ears. Silas was right. She had deserved an explanation, but now that she had one, she couldn't begin to process how to feel.

Her voice was soft when she spoke again. "Why are you telling me this now, after all this time?" She couldn't tell him how seeing him was opening fresh wounds, stirring a longing in her heart for the happy times when they had been blissfully in love.

Silas shifted his weight from one leg to the other. "I don't have a lot of regrets in life, but leaving you like that? That is my biggest regret. I guess I wanted to clear the air, even if my apology is coming far too late to matter."

A wall fell across Hope's heart while she straightened up. She needed to get out of there. "Thanks for coming. My mind is spinning right now, but it's good to have some answers." She paused, rubbing the cast on her arm while she weighed her final words. "Whatever happened in the past, we were good together. That's what I try to remember when I think about you."

She was leaving him with kind words because she couldn't find the energy to stay mad. Not when he had been an eighteen-year-old kid with no life experience to guide him. It sounded like he had been in an impossible situation. Would she have acted any differently if their roles were reversed?

Silas ran a hand through his hair before thumping the railing with his knuckles. "Take care, Hope."

"You too, Silas."

Hope stood on the porch, waiting until Silas climbed into his car before she let the tears fall. He had brought understanding, but there was no way to go back in time to tell her teenage self that life would get better. All the young Hope knew was that her heart had been shattered and she would probably never love anyone again.

The mature Hope was able to look at things through the lens of a woman who had seen some rough years, but also many, many good ones. She closed her eyes, wiping away the final tears before she headed into the house. Silas Foster would never make her cry again.

Monroe was waiting inside, lines of worry drawing his lips down into a frown. "I was going to come rescue you, but Bree said to wait."

Bree was standing still, for once. "What did Silas say?"

She had only been eleven when Silas broke Hope's heart. That was too young to fully grasp how it felt to be in love. Now Bree was the age Hope had been when Silas left. Hope couldn't imagine anyone hurting her sister like that.

"He didn't say much." It was true. The conversation had been brief, but good in the end. "Mostly I think he wanted to apologize."

Monroe's warm eyes studied Hope's face. "Are you okay?"

She could hide the tears from her sister, but Monroe knew her too well. He knew she wasn't okay, but he wouldn't be sure how deep the injuries ran. She wanted to talk to him alone.

"I told my mom I'd pick out a puzzle to work on while my arm is healing. Do you want to help me pick it out?"

Bree made a face, scrunching her nose. "Ewe. Puzzles. Ick." She headed towards the kitchen, leaving Hope alone with Monroe.

His arm circled her shoulders, and he pressed her to his side. "Do you want to talk about it?"

Hope turned her cheek into Monroe's chest, muffling her words. "All I wanted, all these years, was to understand why he left me like he did. Turns out, he had a daughter with his ex-girlfriend."

Monroe's sharp hiss of breath tickled her ear.

"She didn't tell him she was pregnant until months later, and when she finally did, she swore him to secrecy."

"That must have been an impossible situation."

Monroe's deep voice rumbled in his chest. His hand stroked her back and tears burned hot in her eyes.

This time, she allowed them to fall.

"Is it stupid to say that I feel completely betrayed?"

Monroe pressed his warm hand against her cheek. "Did you love him?"

"I did."

"Then no, it isn't strange that you feel betrayed. I've seen you give your heart away over the years. You love deeply, and you are all in when you fall. How could you have possibly been prepared for a blow like that?"

Hope wrapped her good arm around Monroe's waist, taking comfort in his strong arms. This wasn't the first time he had comforted her, and it certainly wouldn't be the last. She closed her eyes, letting herself imagine, just for a minute, that the arms wrapped around her wanted something more than friendship.

As quickly as the idea came, it was replaced by Silas's face. Hope knew, in the deepest corners of her heart, that given a choice, she'd choose Silas. That was why, as comforting as Monroe's arms were, Hope pushed back.

There was a fine line between friendship and love. Hope refused to blur that line with Monroe. He was too valuable as a friend.

They picked out a puzzle from a deep closet in the basement. Hope studied the chickens on the front, pecking the ground with their little beaks. The thousand colorful pieces would distract her nicely until she could forget about the handsome heartbreaker who lived across town.

That's what she told herself when she began sorting pieces. And that's what she told herself when she brushed her teeth before bed. It wasn't until she was pulling up the covers around her chin that she allowed herself the chance to fully process Silas's words.

He hadn't wanted to leave her.

It brought a quiver to her heart. If he hadn't wanted to leave, did that mean he had loved her when he'd gone? More importantly, was there a chance he loved her still?

She closed her eyes and let her heart imagine, just for a moment, how life would have been if Silas had never left. She was picturing their wedding day when she finally drifted off to sleep, a sad smile tugging at her lips.

CHAPTER 8

Much as Silas tried to hide it, there was something on his face when he got home that drew Sierra's attention.

"Why are you sad, Daddy?" she had asked. She was dressed in her pajamas, yawning widely while she climbed into bed.

He reached out to smooth her hair. "I'm okay. I just talked to a friend that reminded me about how hard it is to be a grown up sometimes." He placed his hands on his hips, his lips curling into a teasing grin. "You're not planning on growing up, right?"

Sierra giggled. "I'm going to keep growing until I'm as tall as you." She stretched her hand high in the air.

"I certainly hope not. How will I be able to give you piggyback rides if you are as tall as me?" Silas tickled her side and she shrieked, lunging away before she lay back on her pillow.

Of all the things he had said to Hope, the one thing that would never change was how grateful he was to have Sierra. She was sunshine and brightness even through her physical struggles.

"How are the tummy goblins tonight?" He watched Sierra's face, waiting for it to scrunch up in pain, but her expression was smooth.

"No goblins. I think Grandma made me better."

"Oh, really?" Silas reached for a blanket, pulling it up to her chin. "How did she do that?"

Sierra's eyes lit up. "Ice cream. Grandma says her ice cream is filled with magic."

"Well then, you'd better keep eating it." Silas reached for a book, pulling it off the end table. He flipped it open to a chapter and then paused, letting his hand hold the pages in place. "Pumpkin, how do you like being here?"

Joy poured from Sierra's voice as she talked. She loved getting to see her cousins, and her grandma and grandpa. She wanted to keep running in the backyard and letting Grandpa show her butterflies. She loved helping Grandma make cookies in the kitchen. The words spilled out of her with excitement, each word cutting deeply into his soul.

Silas had a good job in the city. The pay was high, and the hours were flexible, which gave him time to spend with Sierra when she was sick. But he couldn't ignore the fact that in the few short days he had been home, there was more color to her cheeks than he had seen in months. If she kept improving, he was going to have to seriously consider moving back to the country.

The thought of uprooting their lives and starting over gave him a pang, but he knew he'd do anything for her. Even if it meant giving up everything in his comfort zone.

A tug on his arm reminded him that he had a book to read. He kissed the top of Sierra's head and read until her eyes were drooping. She reached for Simmy, pulling the cat to her chest. Silas tucked Coco the monkey beside her and smoothed down the covers. Sierra was snoring softly when he turned the lights off.

Making his way downstairs, Silas began to rummage through the fridge. He opened the container and sniffed the food inside. It smelled fresh enough. The lasagna was turning in the microwave when Rose wandered into the kitchen.

"How did your errand go?"

Silas appraised his sister. She wouldn't be asking if she didn't know something. That meant their mom had been talking about him again.

"What did mom tell you?" The microwave beeped and Silas pulled his plate out, taking it to the table.

"Just that you were heading out to return a platter." She grabbed two forks out of the drawer, handing one to Silas. "You just returned a platter to one of her friends, right? Or am I missing something?"

A sigh escaped Silas's mouth as he sat at the table. He usually told Rose everything, but tonight he hesitated. He took a bite of the lasagna, playfully swatting at Rose's hand when she reached for her own bite.

"Do you want me to make you a plate?" He asked the

question, knowing full well she'd say no. Sure enough, she shook her head.

"I just wanted a little taste."

Silas hid a smile. Even though Rose was married now, and a mom with responsibilities of her own, she still acted like a little sister.

"Where's Keaton?"

Rose glanced towards the door. "He was putting the girls down. I asked them if they wanted to go home and sleep in their own beds, but they were too excited about getting to sleep here. Anyway." She reached for another bite. "You were going to tell me what the big deal is about this platter, right?"

Silas groaned. He could easily evade the question, but the truth was that he desperately wanted someone to talk to. Rose happened to be a fabulous listener.

He shoveled another bite of lasagna in his mouth, trying to keep his expression neutral. "It's fun watching our girls hang out. Sierra is loving it here."

Rose swatted his arm. "Nice try. Spill it."

Silas knew when to give up. "This stays between us, okay?"

"Cross my heart." Rose set her fork on the table, as if sensing that it was time to be more serious.

"I went to see Hope."

Rose's mouth dropped open. "Hope Matthews?"

He nodded. "Yeah."

"I thought mom said you were returning a platter." She twisted her wedding ring on her finger.

Silas pushed his plate away. "I took it back to the Matthews Ranch and handed it to Bree. Then, instead of walking away like a sane person, I asked to see Hope." He could still feel the jitters from standing on that porch.

Rose's eyes were wide. "How did it go?" She had been a junior in high school when Silas left. He knew she saw firsthand the explosion he left in his wake. Hope's sadness couldn't have been easy to watch.

"I don't know." Silas pulled a hand across his brow, replaying their conversation in his mind. "I apologized for the way I left her."

"How did she take it?"

Silas closed his eyes, picturing her face. "It's hard to tell. I thought if I explained what happened, we'd find some sort of closure. I don't know if we can get that, though. I mean, she said I didn't need to apologize, but I feel awful."

He paused, trying to put his feelings into words. "When you don't see someone for years, it is easy to change the narrative. I thought I'd moved on from her years ago but seeing her brought all the memories to the surface. I know I'm a mature adult now, but talking to her made me feel like I was in high school again."

"Do you still love her?" As usual, Rose was getting right to the point.

"Yes." The words fell easily from his lips. "I wish I didn't."

Rose nodded, her face grim. "So, what do you want to do?"

"Short of inventing a time machine? I don't know."

* * *

SILAS EXPECTED that working remotely was going to be difficult, but he was settling into a routine. One week into their visit, and he had already set up a small space in the family room that let him work while keeping an eye out for Sierra. Between webcams and noise canceling headphones, Silas had been able to keep up with all the demands of his job.

He could even begrudgingly admit that it was way easier to take care of Sierra when she had cousins to run around with and loving grandparents who spent hours playing with their granddaughters. Silas kept waiting for Sierra's stomach to give her problems, but she had only had one bad night since they had been home. It made him reluctant to return to the city any time soon.

The door barged open when Silas was pressing send on a report. He leaned back from the computer to watch Sierra, Lacy and Chrissy running towards him.

"Can Sierra come to class with us today?" Lacy was tugging at his hand.

Chrissy bounced on her toes. "Mom said yes, but we have to ask you."

Silas didn't need to ask Sierra what her answer would be. Her eyes were bright with excitement. The girls had been talking about seeing animals all week.

"Let's talk to Aunt Rose." Silas pushed his office chair in, turning his computer screen off.

He found his sister in her van, already buckling in the extra booster seat for Sierra.

"How did you know I'd say yes?" Silas asked.

"Um, because it's a ranch. You like animals just as much as I do." Rose blew a strand off her face when she stood. "She's going to love it."

"Are you sure their teacher will be okay with you bringing an extra child?"

Rose looked away, not quite meeting his eyes. "I asked last week, and she said it was fine."

There was something in her tone that sounded off. Silas lifted an eyebrow. "So, what aren't you telling me?"

The sun beat down on them with a reminder that they were in the thick of the summer months. Rose wiped a hand across her brow. "Bree Matthews is their teacher. It's at the family ranch." She glanced at Silas's face, and then down at her hands. "I can take the girls. I know you like to go places with Sierra, but she'll be happy with us. You don't need to come."

Silas waited for the gaping hole in his gut to open but it didn't come. Instead, there was a small pit, with discomfort flickering around the edges. He shook his head, smiling softly. "I think I'll be okay going there. I had my awkward conversation with Hope yesterday. Now, maybe we can be friends. Besides, we're going to see Bree, not Hope. Right?"

"Right." Rose's shoulders relaxed. "Let's get the girls."

If there was a tightness in Silas's chest when they turned onto Old Ranch Road, he chose to ignore it. Instead, he focused on the soft laughter coming from the back seat, where the cousins were chattering away. He hadn't realized how heavy his heart had been watching Sierra in pain. Now, for the first time in as long as he could remember, she was acting like a healthy child.

For that, Silas would be willing to give up anything. He took a small cleansing breath, letting out a sigh of relief when Rose pulled past the main house and drove up around the hill. A sprawling horse pasture opened before them, with horses grazing nearby. Off to one side of the pasture, dirt had been compacted down and fenced in, forming a small arena outside a horse barn.

A lone figure stood at the edge of the arena. Silas's heart began to thump an uneven beat until she turned, and he realized he wasn't looking at Hope, but Bree. Her face lit up when she looked at the girls.

"Hi Lacy and Chrissy. Who did you bring with you today?" Bree bent down so she could see Sierra's face.

"I'm Sierra." Sierra was shy when she spoke. She slid to the side so she was partway obscured by her dad's leg.

"Hi Sierra. I'm glad you came with your cousins today. Do you like horses?"

Silas could feel her nodding into the back of his leg. He knelt down beside his daughter, putting a comforting arm around her shoulders.

Bree was waiting patiently, a welcoming smile on her lips. She glanced at Silas, and then back at Sierra.

Sierra nodded yes again, this time so everyone could see.

Bree held her hand out for a high five. "I like them, too.

Today, I thought I could introduce you to a couple of my favorite horses. What do you think?"

"Yes!" the girls chorused, their voices high with excitement.

Silas gave Sierra a reassuring squeeze and gently pushed her forward. He watched as they walked to the fence, where a trio of horses were grazing. They were petting one of the horse's noses when Silas noticed a movement out of the corner of his eye.

A woman emerged from the barn, leading a horse towards Bree. A hat shaded her face from the sun, but the cast on her arm gave her away. Silas clenched his fists against the wave of longing that shot through his body. So much for the closure he thought he had. He assumed Hope would be elsewhere on the ranch.

Silas could feel his stomach turning on itself when he wrenched his attention back to his daughter. He had maybe a minute to compose himself before Hope would be there.

Sierra was the distraction he needed. A smile lifted her cheeks while she held her small hand out in front of the horse. He bumped his nose against her hand and she shrieked, letting out a full laugh.

"He likes me," Sierra said.

"He definitely does." Bree stood between the girls. "Are you ready to learn how we take care of these guys?"

"Yes." Sierra was standing up straight, her shyness gone.

Bree waved to Hope. "I have some friends here today."

Hope grinned. "I heard these were extra special

helpers."

"They are the best." Bree led the girls forward, introducing each of them. Then she turned to the parents. "This is Rose and, uh, I think you know Silas."

Silas was put on the spot, aware of the eyes that watched him.

"Hi, Hope. It's good to see you again." It was one thing to stand on a porch, apologizing for hurts from the past. It was another thing completely to act casual when his heart threatened to thump out of his chest.

Silas sat through an entire lesson on how to take care of horses, including the various parts of a saddle and what they did. His mind was unable to focus on any of the words. By the time the sisters were done teaching their lesson, Silas knew he had a choice to make.

The girls ran for the van, but Silas hung back. "Thanks for the lesson, Bree. Sierra's going to be talking about this for a long time."

"She's a sweetheart." Bree glanced at her sister and then reached for the reins. "I'm going to go get the gear off this guy."

Hope made a move to follow, but Silas held his hand out, lightly resting it on her arm. His words, so carefully chosen, died on his lips. He wanted to act cool, like seeing his ex didn't phase him, but he knew that would be a lie.

"Can I take you to dinner?" he blurted.

An eternity passed before a smile lifted the corners of her mouth.

"I think I'd like that."

CHAPTER 9

Bree was waiting to pounce as soon as Hope walked into the barn. Hope paused in the doorway, letting her heart settle.

"What happened out there?" Bree asked, bouncing on the tips of her toes. She was clearly excited for her sister.

"Nothing much. He asked me on a date and I said yes."

Bree's loud shrieks echoed through the barn, causing the horse she was brushing to rear back in alarm. She pressed a hand to his side. "Sorry, Vero. Easy does it, bud."

Dust motes swirled in the air while the horse calmed down. He was one of their gentlest horses, which was why Hope had brought him out when Bree was ready. She reached for a sugar cube, watching him smack his lips as he gulped it down.

"Do you think I'm making a mistake?" Hope leaned against the stall.

"Why would you think that?"

"I don't know. I'm second guessing how wise it would be to start something with him when I know I'm heading back to the city soon. But he didn't ask me to marry him. He asked me to dinner. What's the worst that can happen?"

Bree shook her head, rolling her eyes. "Let's see. The worst that can happen is you'll fall head over heels in love and he'll break your heart." She planted her hands on her hips while trying not to smile. "Oh, wait. He already did that."

"Harsh." Hope rubbed the back of her neck. "But you're right. I've already cried plenty of tears over Silas Foster. I don't need to cry any more."

Bree hung the reins on a hook and closed the stall door behind her. "Do you think you guys can be friends after everything that's happened?"

"I'd like to think so. I'm not sure."

The question hung in the back of Hope's mind for the rest of the day. Seeing Silas in the doctor's office had been as shocking as her fall. The pains of both had lanced through her body, piercing both her arm and her heart.

Did he deserve any more of her time? He felt justified in leaving her behind. Even though he had been put in a difficult situation, if he truly had cared for her, he could have found a way to say goodbye. A note of some kind would have softened the blow.

So why was Hope agreeing to meet him for dinner? She had to admit that she wanted to know how Silas's life had turned out. He had been the most important person in her life at one time. It was clear that he had a daughter, but she really didn't know anything else about him. She told herself it was idle curiosity that kept her interested.

Hope was brushing on a thin coat of lip gloss when she realized why she had really said yes. She was still connected to Silas by strings that stretched taut over the years. No matter how hard she tried to push the feelings down, she had to admit that a part of her was still in love with him.

Did first love ever truly die? Was there always going to be a shadow of Silas on her heart? She owed it to herself to try to sever all those strings so she could head back to the city with no attachments.

By the time the doorbell rang, Hope was completely calm. She opened the door to find Silas, dressed in a navy button down shirt and slacks. His hair curled softly to one side, a small chunk of hair refusing to curl the same direction as the rest.

The years may have been emotionally rough for Silas, but physically, they had done him well. His shoulders filled out the shirt, hinting at muscles that spanned his shoulders. The dusting of stubble along his jaw highlighted angled cheek bones.

And yet, somehow, Hope could still see traces of the young man she had given her heart to. His eyes were the same color of blue; the turquoise of the ocean as the sun set over the water. And his lips curled into a smile that she would recognize anywhere.

The man in front of her was as familiar as he was

foreign, and she suddenly felt shy. Her blood raced through her veins.

"You look incredible," Silas said.

Hope smiled while she held up her arm. "Do you know how hard it is to coordinate with a cast? I can't wait to get it off." She had ended up going with a simple white blouse and a short tan skirt, finishing the outfit off with dark red ankle boots. Her hair hung loose on her shoulders, softly curling in waves.

The appraising look Silas gave as he eyed her up and down kick started the butterflies in her stomach. She knew what it felt like to be adored by this man. She also knew what it felt like to be abandoned. With a quick roll of her shoulders, Hope shook off any romantic thoughts she had. The purpose of tonight's date was to place Silas firmly in the friend zone.

She climbed into his car, glancing back where Sierra's booster seat was visible in the back seat. It was the visible reminder that a lot had changed over the years with Silas. His eyes had the same depth, but he was a completely different man than the young man she had known years before.

Hope expected there to be an awkward tension in the drive, but as soon as the car turned on, the radio began blasting a song that Hope recognized from the past.

She glanced at Silas, waiting for him to begin his dancing. Sure enough, as soon as the song got to the chorus, he was tapping his fingers on the steering wheel and bobbing his head. Hope filled her lungs with air and began to sing. The look he shot her was pure delight.

By the time they pulled up to the restaurant, her cheeks were pink from laughter. She climbed out of the seat and met Silas at the front of the car, a grin on her face.

"Are you ever going to let me open the door for you?" Silas teased.

"Probably not." With that, she grabbed his arm, sliding her hand towards his before freezing. It was a gesture as familiar as breathing, but she hadn't stopped to think what she was doing. The next step would be to wrap her fingers in his, and he'd lift her hand to his lips.

Hope awkwardly let go before she reached his wrist. She hadn't realized how ingrained some habits were. "Sorry," she said.

"It's what we used to do. I know." He placed a hand on her back, guiding her towards the door. "I'll be honest. I almost canceled on you a bunch of times."

Hope looked up at that, her heart contracting. For as casual as she had pretended to be about the date, she knew she would have been upset if he had bailed.

"Why?"

Silas rocked back on his heels, gesturing in Hope's direction. "Because you're you, and I'm still just me. You are taking the world by storm, whereas my world has gotten a lot smaller with Sierra in it. I feel like you're on a completely different planet than me, even though we're standing side by side."

Hope wasn't sure how to respond. Was it possible that Silas was going to be completely open with her? She closed her eyes and thought about their past. Honesty had never been one of his problems, until the day he left.

"I may be aiming for a much larger stage, but singing makes me a small part of someone else's world. Ideally, people will come to watch me perform and leave with their hearts a bit lighter. Then they'll get back to their normal lives. You're the center of someone else's universe right now, and will be forever. I think that makes you pretty impressive."

They stepped up to the hostess booth, where the woman grabbed two menus and led them to the table. A bright blue flier was tucked in between the condiments. Hope picked it up, holding it gingerly between her fingers while she read the advertisement. She began to laugh, which caused Silas to raise an eyebrow.

"What's so funny about the flier?"

Hope pointed to the microphone on the front, with the open call for auditions. "Did you know I recorded a few songs for this diner after I headed to college? I got my start following a flier like this."

"Seriously?" Silas ran a hand through his hair. "I was gone by then, but it would have been surreal to hear your voice when I sat down to eat. What are you planning now with your music?"

"I was hoping to go on tour with the Ginny Brooks band, but I got the word last night that they went with someone else." Hope's face flushed. "I don't think anyone is surprised, given the way I bombed that audition."

"What happened?" Silas looked up from the menu.

Hope held up her cast. "This. I slipped on a bead and fell flat on my butt before I even sang a note." She let out a small laugh. "In school they taught us to make ourselves memorable at auditions, but somehow, I don't think making an utter fool of yourself is what they meant."

She was laughing now, but Silas had a frown on his face. "Were you able to sing at all?"

Hope nodded. "I personally thought I faked it pretty well. I held it together until I was off the stage. Then Monroe took me to the doctor."

"And that's where I saw you."

Weight filled the room, an invisible force squeezing against Hope's heart. She had felt the heaviness ever since the day she saw Silas. Even now, her heart struggled to beat, as if each throb was laced through with the painful memories that the man in front of her had left her behind.

Her voice was soft when she spoke. She weighed her words, unsure how much to open up. Then she decided it didn't matter. If there was any chance of staying friends with Silas, she needed to tell him everything on her mind.

"I felt like I had been struck by lightning when I saw you. I'm pretty sure the jolt of it would have knocked me to my knees if I wasn't already sitting in the chair."

Silas nodded. "I know what you mean."

"I never thought I'd see you again, and when I did, I was

taken away so quickly, there wasn't time to react. I don't actually know why you were at the doctor's office that day."

He ran a hand through his hair, the gesture as familiar to Hope as her own breath. She knew how it felt to run her own hands through his hair. He'd mess it up, and she'd try to straighten back the curls that escaped.

"It was Sierra. We were doing blood work again."

That was news to Hope. She had figured it was a routine checkup. "Is she okay?"

Silas looked at Hope in such a way, she figured she had overstepped her boundaries somehow. She cleared her throat. "Sorry. That's none of my business."

Silas gave a small shake of his head. "It's not that. You are welcome to ask. I'm just surprised you'd want to know about her."

"Why wouldn't I? She's part of your life. If she's important to you, which clearly she is, I'd like to hear more."

Hope meant her words. She could judge Silas all day long for choosing his daughter over her, but if the roles were reversed, wouldn't she have done the same? It didn't make sense to hold a grudge against a young child.

As Silas began to speak, Hope said a silent prayer that the Lord would let her heart be open. She wanted healing for both of them. Hope watched Silas's face while he spoke, the love in his eyes radiating when he said Sierra's name.

She heard the heartache in Silas's words as he spoke about Sierra's illness. There was frustration with doctors mixed with a level of respect that they were all working together to find a solution.

Hope let Silas talk through dinner, deflecting his questions back to him any time he tried to change the subject. She wasn't sure how, but hearing his love for his daughter was helping to knit her heart back together. The strings that tied her to Silas slowly unraveled while she set her frustration and anger free.

Silas looked up when the waitress brought them the check. His face fell. "I can't believe I spent our whole dinner talking about Sierra. You didn't need to know about her doctors or ballet lessons or any of it. I didn't get to hear anything about you."

He was right. He had dominated the conversation, but that was how Hope had wanted it to be. "I was asking you the questions."

"Yeah, but I could have been more aware." Silas slumped back in his seat. "I haven't taken anyone out in so long, I forgot how to be a good date. Sorry."

Hope reached for his fingers, covering them with her hand. "Sierra is your life. I wanted to know about her." She bit the side of her cheek. "I wanted to understand why you left me, and now I do. It's a good thing. She sounds amazing."

"She really is." Silas flipped his fingers up so he could brush them against Hope's hand. "My heart never belonged to Zoe, but as soon as I met Sierra, I was a goner. She was the only thing stronger than my tie to you."

Tingles raced up Hope's arm. She closed her eyes

against the flutters that swirled around her heart. Sitting with Silas, Hope found the healing she had been seeking.

"She's lucky to have you for a dad." Hope drew her hand back and folded it in her lap. It was time to end their date before Silas wrapped any new strings around her heart.

CHAPTER 10

Silas snuck glances at Hope the entire drive home. He had always thought she was beautiful, but now he couldn't keep his eyes off of her. Somehow, even through his mistakes of the past, she found ways to make him feel like he was okay just the way he was.

It was one thing to admire a person from afar. It was another, completely, to get to spend time with a person and see their true worth. Silas was grateful that their paths had crossed again.

He pulled the car into the front of Hope's house and set it in park. "I know I can't open your door for you, but can I walk you to your porch?"

Keeping a straight face while asking the question was difficult. Especially when the corner of Hope's mouth twitched upward when she turned to face him.

Not opening Hope's door was something they had started when they were in high school. One of the more popular teachers had taught the boys how to be gentlemen, including opening doors for the ladies. Over the next couple of weeks, there was a line of people waiting to go through any open door, with everyone wanting to hold the door open for someone else.

One day, when late to class because of people messing around, Hope stormed into the room and sank down beside Silas. "I swear, if one more person tries to open a door for me, I might lose my mind."

Silas took her words to heart, and left her sitting in the car when he pulled in front of her house that day after school. He walked to the porch, waiting for the angry shriek he was sure to follow when she realized he was ignoring her. Instead, a minute later, he was tackled from behind in a giant hug.

"You listened," she said.

"I'll always listen." Silas kissed Hope's upturned mouth and promised to never open another door for her until she asked him to.

It was a little joke between them, but Silas was glad to see that some things stayed the same. Hope pushed open her door. "Never on the doors, but yes, you can walk me to the porch."

Nerves swirled in tight circles in Silas's stomach when he got to the bottom of the steps. He licked the edge of his lips, his mouth dry. Walking Hope to the door was something he had done dozens of times, but this time was different.

As a teenager, there was always the flutter of excitement before Silas would kiss Hope goodnight. Now, he wasn't quite sure what to do. He wasn't sure how to act now that they were just friends. Especially when the desire to kiss her was just as strong as it had been back then.

"Thanks for being open with me, tonight." Hope leaned against the railing near the bottom step, her dark hair blending in with the night.

"I'm glad we did this." Silas slid his hands into his back pockets. "I needed to talk to you. I needed to clear the air."

Hope's body froze and Silas was afraid he had said something wrong. Then she smiled. "I really needed this, too."

She walked up the remaining steps and Silas followed. He held his hand out to shake hers. She paused for a second before she moved it to the side, stepping forward to press her cheek against his chest. Her hand brushed against his stomach before it slid to his back.

Silas wasted no time in wrapping his arms around her. She fit against him more perfectly than he remembered. He lowered his face, breathing in the scent of her citrus shampoo, trying to lock every part of this experience to memory. The way the wind blew her hair up to tickle his cheeks. The way heat raced through his body when she pressed her hand to the small of his back.

He memorized the way her head tucked against his chest, his heart thumping when he tucked a strand of hair behind her ear. She was close enough for him to hear the hitch in her breath when his hand paused on her cheek. All it would take was a few inches and he could press his lips to hers. It was something he had dreamt about for years when the memory of their last moments together started to fade.

Silas closed his eyes and let his heart sink into the moment, capturing every detail before he stepped back, reluctantly lowering his arms. He no longer had the right to kiss Hope Matthews, no matter how much he ached to.

"Take care, Hope." He watched her turn for the door, waiting for her to turn back around to wave like she always did.

"Goodnight, Silas." With that, she was stepping into the house and away from his arms.

Silas waited until the door gave a soft click before he started down the steps. He paused on the bottom step, reaching underneath the railing to run his fingers across the inscription. They might not be H + S anymore, but Hope would always hold a special place in his heart.

He drove into the night, feeling lighter than he had in years. There was no magic wand that would erase the hurts of the past, but talking to Hope had been a blessing. Hopefully he could move on now, with a clear heart and mind. He'd be ready when his next great love came along.

All the lights in the house were off except a light in the entryway when Silas got home. He walked into the house, feeling a sense of foreboding while he waited for his eyes to adjust to the dim light. Sure enough, the silhouette of his mom sat on the couch, hunched over a small figure.

She looked up when Silas approached, raising a finger to her lips. Sierra's hair spilled across his mom's lap, loose from the ponytails she usually wore.

Silas quickened his pace, heading for his daughter, but his mom held out her hand. "She's okay," she whispered.

It didn't take a detective to figure out what was wrong. A heating pad was draped across Sierra's stomach, and there were tea cups on the table. Dried tear streaks ran down her face.

"Why didn't you call me?" A fist was clenching Silas's heart where he stood. He had no right to be out with Hope when his daughter had needed him at home.

Mom Foster patted the cushion next to her. "Because we had it handled."

Silas sat, reluctantly allowing his mom to keep holding his daughter. He brought his hand over and rested it in Sierra's hair. "You should have called."

His mom rested her hand over his. "You weren't the easiest of my teenagers to raise. Did you know that?"

The change in subject was strange. Silas smirked. "That's an understatement."

"I think your dad and I said and did all the wrong things when you announced that you were moving to the city a few weeks before graduation. Your actions made no sense."

She slid her hand to Sierra's forehead, brushing the hair back from her face. "I know you had your reasons, but I don't think I was nearly as supportive as I could have been. I've been trying to make up for that."

Silas sat up straight. "None of us knew what we were doing. I don't blame you for that."

"I know, and I appreciate it. You asked why I didn't call you." Her voice grew soft. "You told me, years ago, that you had broken up with Hope Matthews. I had no reason to believe she was anything other than a fleeting high school crush. But then I saw the shock on your face when I called you over to say hi to her at the barbeque. That wasn't the look of a man greeting an old friend. You looked like you were seeing a ghost."

So much for keeping things private from his family. His face was too easy to read. Silas cupped a hand to the back of his neck. "I never thought I'd see her again."

"I could tell."

Sierra shifted in her sleep, curling onto her side. She mumbled something and then pulled Simmy close. Silas held his breath as she settled back into a slow and steady pattern of breathing.

"Silas, I knew tonight was important. I don't know how you ended things with Hope back then, or how you left them tonight. I thought you deserved the chance to make things right."

She reached for a blanket, pulling it closer to Sierra's chin. "Besides, I hoped you'd have fun. Sierra's tummy was hurting her but she calmed down quickly. I knew she'd be okay."

The frustration in Silas's heart began to fade. It had

been so long since anyone had taken care of him, he had forgotten how good it felt. "Thanks, Mom. I can take her now."

Mom Foster leaned back against the cushions. "Why don't you get ready for bed? I'm okay sitting with her a while longer. You can grab her when you're ready to settle down."

Silas hesitated for just a minute before nodding. He stood, pausing in the doorway. "You were right about Hope, Mom. We needed tonight."

"I'm glad."

The floorboards creaked when Silas headed upstairs to start his bedtime routine. Moonlight cast shadows from tree branches onto the wall. They gently swayed back and forth, and Silas took a moment to watch them. His life had started like those branches, gently buffeted by small breezes, before it got complicated. Now, he felt like he was running from one storm to the next. It felt good to let his guard down, even if just for a few hours.

He found his mom nodding off to sleep when he came downstairs. Her head drooped downwards, towards Sierra's, and a wave of gratitude surged through Silas. He was thankful to have her in such a safe space.

Silas woke his mom, gently pressing a hand down on her shoulder. Then he took Sierra, curling her to his chest while he carried her to the guest room. He settled her onto one side of the bed before slipping under the covers on the other.

It was well past midnight before Silas was ready to

sleep. The last thought on his mind before he drifted off was how good it had felt to hold Hope in his arms once again.

* * *

IN THE MORNING, all traces of Sierra's stomach ache from the night before had vanished. She chased Lacy and Chrissy in the backyard, her laughter and smiles bright. Silas looked on with a heart filled with gratitude. His mom had been right. Sierra was fine.

A loud thumping sound drew Silas's attention to the garage. He found his dad and Keaton hammering away at a wagon. Large wooden sunflowers of various sizes lay scattered across the ground. A memory flashed back to Silas of standing in the back of the wagon, throwing candy at strangers down a parade route. That year, he had been dressed as a honey bee.

"Let me guess. This is your float for the parade?" An early morning parade heralded in the start of Strawberry Days for Elk Mountain. It was a town celebration that lasted for a week, with vendor booths and live music at the library park.

Keaton stapled a plastic leaf to the side of the wagon. "Yep. The theme this year is Spreading Sunshine. The girls are so excited to participate."

Every summer, families and businesses from around town gathered for the parade. It was said that everyone who participated would have a good harvest for the year to come. There were only a few big ranching families left in the town who actually cared about harvest season, but the tradition remained.

"Do you want any help?" Silas asked. Four hours later, he regretted ever asking the question. His hands ached when he stepped back to observe their work.

The sunflowers were now attached to the outside of the wagon, the paint still drying on a few of the petals. A short, green bench sat in the center with room for people to sit.

Only one thing remained. Silas and Keaton helped hook the wagon up to the tractor. Then Grandpa Foster took his granddaughters for a slow ride down the driveway. He did a wide u-turn and brought the wagon back to the front of the house amidst peals of laughter.

"How's our time?" he asked.

Keaton glanced at his watch. "We've still got a few hours until dinner time. It should be just enough time to check on Silas's costume."

Silas snapped his eyes away from the handle he was attaching to the inside of the wagon. "Excuse me?"

"You didn't think we'd march in the parade without you, did you?" Keaton's eyes held an apology.

"It's a family tradition, Silas." His dad rubbed a hand across his forehead. "Besides, we thought you'd want to walk with Sierra."

Silas had to agree that they were right. That was why he found himself, two days later, driving to the center of town wearing a bright yellow shirt while he held a sunflower hood in his lap.

Sierra hadn't stopped chattering the entire drive. She and her cousins were dressed in yellow tutus, with green leaves on each shoulder of their leotards. They wore brown headbands that had springs attached to the tops, with little buzzing bees that danced whenever they shook their heads.

The air was electric when Mr. Foster pulled into a large parking lot that had been sectioned off for entries. Silas gave a quick cursory glance of the crowd, but he didn't recognize most of the faces. Some of the floats looked familiar from his childhood, but many of the people driving them were new.

At first, Silas was self-conscious of all the people glancing his way. It took him a second to realize that they weren't staring at him, but at the sunflower headdress he had thrown on so both his hands were free. He had been so worried about shielding Sierra from town gossip, he had forgotten that to most of these people, he was just another random participant in the parade. Out of costume, he'd blend right in.

Silas was lifting Sierra into the wagon when a shadow blocked the sun. Silas glanced over his shoulder to check who was there and immediately groaned.

Hope sat on a gorgeous horse with bright ribbons woven through his black mane. A turquoise hat perched on her head, covering part of the dark braids that fell to either side of her shoulders. She looked incredible, from the tight button up shirt she wore to the light makeup that made her eyes pop.

Silas, on the other hand, looked ridiculous. He wished for a pit in the earth to swallow him whole, but there wasn't one.

"I thought I recognized you. Nice sunflower," Hope said, her mouth twitching.

Silas straightened his shoulders. "I hear all the cool kids are wearing hoods these days." His sheepish grin fell when he registered that she was up on a horse. " Are you allowed to ride with your broken arm?"

She winked. "I won't tell the doctor if you don't."

Silas was looking for a comeback when a voice boomed over a loudspeaker. "Places, everyone."

"That's my cue to join my family. It was good to see you, Silas." With that, she rode off to join the founding families at the front of the parade.

Silas turned to Sierra. "Are you ready to be the cutest sunflower out there?"

In response, she grinned and reached for her bucket of candy. Silas turned his attention to the parade route, knowing that Hope was somewhere ahead of them, dazzling the crowd with her incredible smile. For the first time in years, he was glad to be home.

CHAPTER 11

The parade meandered down the length of Main Street, lined on both sides with throngs of people who clapped and cheered as Hope and the rest of the founding families led the way. She knew that somewhere behind her, dressed in a ridiculous sunflower hood, was the man who brought a smile to her face.

She had no claim on Silas anymore, and yet, as soon as the horses were put away, Hope made her way to the library grounds, just to see if she could catch a glimpse of him.

Every now and then, she caught a flash of yellow in the crowd, but by the time she made her way through the press of people, it was gone. With each false sighting, her face fell. This wasn't the way she had anticipated spending the day, her heart fluttering at the thought of running into Silas again.

Going to dinner with him had unlocked something in

her. Sure, there were the complicated layers of high school memories, but beneath it all, there was the boy who had won her heart, all those years ago. The laughter he brought to the surface. The way she could completely be herself, walls down, when most of her days were spent trying to impress other people.

Hope gave a futile scan of the park once more, and then headed towards the raised concrete patio at the back of the library that was being used as a stage. A woman cleared her voice and tapped the microphone. "Can everyone hear me?"

The crowd barely stopped moving, but a few people stopped in their tracks, turning to face the stage. Locals knew that there would be live entertainment all day as musicians, dance studios, and students took turns showcasing numbers they had been working on. It was a distraction in the background. People cycled through the few rows of folding chairs that were set up to provide a place to rest.

Hope watched as a young girl took the stage and strains of an Irish jig began to play over the loudspeakers. The girl was light on her feet while she danced around the stage in an intricate pattern, her golden pigtails flying out to the side while her kilt swayed to the music. Before long, a young boy joined her. They weren't professional dancers by any stretch, but Hope knew how they'd feel leaving the stage. It was incredible to have a crowd applauding you for a job well done.

The efforts to find Silas weren't panning out. Maybe he had gone home, and she was wasting her time looking for him. She sank into a folding chair, half heartedly watching a juggler while she questioned her motives. What did it matter if she saw Silas again? They weren't going to start a relationship.

She realized that she wanted a chance to talk to him with all the pressures gone. During dinner, there had been a weight to the conversation. Things needed to be said, and the air had to be cleared. Now that they had done that, Hope wanted something light. She wanted to hear more about Silas's normal life.

A young man with a violin took the stage, and Hope realized she could let her need for control go. She could put her day in fate's hands. It had been a long time since Hope had performed in an outdoor arena, but she had been singing in front of crowds for years. She might not be able to find Silas, but if she could get on the stage, he'd be able to find her if he wanted to.

Her shoulders tightened as she approached the emcee, breathing a sigh of relief when she realized it was an old friend.

"Hi, Brit," Hope said. "What does the schedule look like today? Any room for me to sing a song?"

Brit's eyes lit up. "You have perfect timing. One of our acts just canceled a few minutes ago. Can you go on in ten?"

The request thudded into her chest and she gulped. Ten minutes wasn't a lot of time to get warmed up and pick a song. Hope nodded. "I can be ready."

She was heading towards the staging area when she

realized she already knew exactly which song she wanted to sing. Ten minutes later, her nerves were calm. She handed over her phone to get plugged into the sound system.

There were no spotlights to bring the focus to her. No thunderous applause when she stepped forward to take the microphone. She hadn't had time to plan an outfit or think about where she'd focus her gaze. Instead, amidst a small spattering of half-hearted cheers, Hope began to sing.

The song started with a rapid beat, the first verse a lament to the busy nature of life. Faces snapped towards Hope as her voice rang out clearly across the park. The more professional performers usually didn't come out until later in the evening. Seats began to fill with curious onlookers, but Silas didn't appear.

Hope sang the chorus, softening her voice as the music slowed to a simple, tender refrain. It spoke of how in the chaos of the world, you could find respite from the storm by turning your faith over to the Lord. She sang each word with conviction, letting faith stir in her own heart.

There was a push and pull to the song, with verses and the chorus warring until the end, when the singer lay their burden down at the Lord's feet. How clearly Hope understood that promise. She had thought breaking her arm was the worst thing that could happen to her. Now she could see that by doing so, the Lord had let her be in the right place to heal wounds from the past.

She wondered how many other times in her life she had been put in the right place by the Lord, but she had been too focused on other things to notice. She had the desire to do better and be better.

There was a brief pause as the last notes of music trailed off before the crowd began to cheer, whistles of approval punctuating the applause. Hope handed the microphone to Brit and turned to give a final wave to the crowd. Her heart skipped a beat when she saw Silas.

He stood to the side of the folded chairs, holding Sierra's hand. A wave of relief shot through her when he gave her a thumbs up. Silas had come like she wished he would.

The closer she got to him, the more her hands began to sweat. What if he was there by accident? He could easily vanish into the crowd before she reached his side.

Hope picked up the pace, only stepping to the side once to let a crowd of laughing teenagers pass. She lost sight of Silas for the briefest moment, and her heart stilled. Then the bright yellow shirt straightened up, and she realized he had been talking to Sierra.

Sierra let go of his hand and melted into the crowd with her cousins, leaving Silas by himself when Hope approached.

She stood in front of Silas, suddenly tongue-tied. Finding him had been such a focus, she had forgotten that she'd actually have to speak to him. She didn't need to worry.

"Man, I've missed hearing you sing," he said.

Silas ran a hand through his hair, pushing his curls the wrong way. Hope tried to let it pass, but old habits were hard to break. She reached out and flicked a stray strand of hair back into place.

"I see you've given up on your dreams of becoming a real sunflower."

Silas cupped the back of his neck. "Too much competition." He shrugged and glanced over his shoulder.

Hope had just found him, but clearly his attention was elsewhere. He scanned the crowd, and then, after a second, turned back to her, a shy smile on his face. "I'm not used to people taking care of Sierra. It's hard to let my guard down."

"Who has her, now?" Hope began to walk towards the vendor booths and Silas fell in step beside her.

"My parents. They are taking the girls to get their faces painted." Silas tucked his hands in his pockets. "Where were you heading next?"

Hope felt the blush creeping up on her cheeks. Her entire goal had been to find Silas, but now that she had, shyness crept in. "Nowhere real. I was hoping I'd bump into you."

Silas stopped walking. "Why?"

Gone were the days of trying to dance around words. If Hope wanted a mature relationship with Silas, she was going to have to speak her mind.

"I guess I was hoping we could talk like friends now. Without our past weighing us down. I want to know more about your life."

"Didn't I already tell you everything last night?" His eyes studied hers.

"That was the serious stuff. I want to know the fun stuff today."

A boy pulling a wagon stopped in front of them, interrupting Silas's reply. He held out a bag of cotton candy. "Need a snack? It's only two dollars."

Silas barely glanced at Hope before he was handing over five dollars. "Two bags, please. Keep the change." He handed a bag to Hope before taking his own. "Do you remember the last time we had cotton candy?"

Hope rolled her eyes. "I'm so glad we're not running the booth that makes this stuff. You were covered in sticky strands of blue sugar."

Silas laughed. "I wasn't sure it would ever wash off, but we did raise a lot of money for the play that year."

They meandered through the booths, pausing every so often to point out some of the more unique items. Hope nibbled on her cotton candy, trying hard to ignore the way Silas's lips smacked as he licked his fingers clean.

The park felt crowded with vendor booths, but before long, they were reaching the final row. Hope's heart sank. She had been enjoying her time with Silas and wasn't ready to have it end.

He met her eyes, and Hope could read the indecision in them. He didn't look like he was ready to say goodbye either. Hope scrambled to find an activity for them to do, but nothing came to mind. She wanted to take him away from the park and find somewhere quiet to talk, but he had come with his family.

She took her time at the last booth, holding out a stuffed unicorn. "Bree would love this."

"Sierra would, too." Silas set it back on the table. "But I don't really want to cart a stuffed animal home."

His words confirmed Hope's worries. Their time together was limited. She set her unicorn down as well. "Good point."

The bubble that Hope had allowed herself to float in came crashing down when Porter appeared in front of her. His face held a look of urgency that made her heart drop.

"What's wrong?" she asked. Silas stilled beside her.

"Nothing's wrong, but we need your help right now." He glanced at Silas, a flicker of recognition widening his eyes. "We could use your help, too."

Silas shrugged and nodded, and one band around Hope's heart loosened. They were going to get more time together. It was replaced by a band of worry. Porter wasn't telling her the entire story.

Porter pulled them to the side and whispered quick instructions before pressing a small object into Hope's hands. Then he was off to grab more siblings.

Silas looked at Hope, his eyes incredulous when she opened her hand to reveal a gleaming diamond ring. "Your brother wasn't playing around."

Hope smiled. "Not Reid. He'd want to make sure Millie has the best of everything."

"Well, I don't want to be the one to mess this up." Silas reached for her hand and pulled her across the wide expanse of the park until they were near the game booths.

He let go, lifting his hand to his forehead as he began to look at each game.

"It's over there," Hope said. She headed towards the fishing booth, trying to ignore the heat that trailed up her arm from Silas's touch.

After a quick conversation with the teens running the booth, Hope found herself crouching down behind a soft curtain. It wasn't until Silas ducked down beside her that she realized how small the space was, and how close his body pressed against hers.

She let out a shaky breath. "Are you sure you're okay with this?"

In response, Silas trailed a finger down her arm. "Absolutely."

He held her gaze, and the air grew thick as Hope studied his face, achingly close to hers. One small breath was all it would take to lean forward and see if their lips remembered how it felt to be together.

She didn't need to ask him how he felt. The soft pressure of his finger as it trailed down her arm left fire in its wake. They were close. Too close. If Hope wasn't careful, the heat roaring through her was going to push her to act before thinking.

She parted her lips to speak, but didn't know what to say. In that moment, she felt like a teenager again, her heart thumping out of her chest as she waited for the boy she loved to finally kiss her.

A light rap on the table beside the booth snapped Hope out of the moment. When the red hook came down, seconds later, Silas was the one who clipped a toy to the string, tugging it gently so the child could pull it back up.

Two more children came through, getting their toys, before Hope heard Reid's voice. Millie's response was filled with laughter. "I can't believe you're making me play all these games."

He murmured something and then their voices were clear. They had stopped at the fishing booth.

The teen in front asked Millie how old she was, just to confirm that she was the right person. And then a green fishing pole was dropping a hook down to Hope and Silas.

Her heart thudded when she held the string tight, letting Silas firmly attach the ring to the end. Then, with a quick tug, the string disappeared over the edge of the fabric.

The world slowed as Hope parted the side of the curtain to peek through.

Reid was down on one knee, the ring held high. Millie's hands covered her mouth while he spoke, but then she was pulling him up, kissing him soundly before shouting yes to the world.

Hope hadn't realized that Silas was watching as well, his head inches from hers, until she leaned back, right into his chest, and an arm flew around her waist to steady her before she crashed to the ground. She rested her head against his chest, willing her heartbeat to slow before she turned to face him.

It was easy to forget that they were sitting in the middle of the town's park, surrounded by throngs of people. Hope knew she should be joining the rest of her family in congratulating the happy couple but her pulse was racing as she leaned in.

Silas was close. So close. She lifted a hand to stroke his cheek. "Thank you."

His response was cut off when Porter's face appeared over the top of the booth. "You did great," he said, completely oblivious that he was saving his sister from potential disaster. Kissing Silas wouldn't be the worst thing in the world, but it would certainly make life more complicated.

Hope couldn't handle complicated right now. She gave Silas a wry smile and stood, turning her attention to her family. She glanced at Silas, who now looked very out of place, and reached for his hand. Her heart settled into a steady beat when he wrapped his fingers around hers with a gentle squeeze. Holding hands with Silas felt right.

Maybe a little complicated wouldn't be so bad.

CHAPTER 12

Selfish, selfish, selfish. This was Hope's moment to spend with her family. Reid and Millie's big moment. And yet, with Hope so close to him, her face inches from his, Silas had almost crossed a line.

He told himself he'd give her just one little kiss. A faint brush of lips to thank her for spending the day with him. But then her brother was looming over the fishing booth and the moment was ruined.

Silas had never felt more relieved in his life. He found himself being pulled forward to congratulate the happy couple. Members of the Matthews family surrounded Reid and Millie on every side as they leaned in to look at the ring.

He forced his attention to focus on Millie, who was beaming while holding out her hand. The diamond on her finger glittered in the sunlight, but the smile on her face shone more brightly.

Reid had an arm protectively draped across her shoulders. This was his fiancé, and he was proud to have her by his side.

Silas hadn't known Reid well. He was a few years older than Hope, and had been off to college when Silas began dating her. Still, there was a message in the glance that Reid threw his way. He may be distracted by the engagement, but he was still a big brother. Silas better not hurt his sister again.

It was that look that threw ice down Silas's back. What had he been thinking? He didn't throw kisses around lightly, and yet, in a moment of weakness, he hadn't taken a second to think about what might happen if he acted on his impulses.

The sound of happy congratulations swirled around Silas but he was sinking into a pit. What had he done? How could he even think about kissing Hope? They weren't lovesick teens anymore. They had lives and responsibilities.

Sierra's face slammed into his mind.

It had been so easy to spend the day with Hope, knowing that Sierra was off with his parents. He had been able to shed the mantle of being a father for long enough to let his heart roam free. Somehow, he had forgotten that there was real life waiting at the end of this day. A daughter who would need to be tucked in, and the ever looming mystery of why she was sick.

Silas pulled back from the happy family, gently tugging Hope with him. "I've got to go," he said. He gave her hand a squeeze and made his way through the crowd, only looking back once to see the confusion on her face. He would have to find a way to explain his actions to her later, but now was not the time.

* * *

SIERRA'S FACE was painted with butterfly wings that stretched high on each cheek. Silas agreed to let her sleep with her face paint on, just this one time, before he kissed her goodnight.

The restlessness kicked in moments later. Silas wasn't ready for sleep. Not yet. He could hear the quiet rise and fall of his parent's voices coming from the family room. They were an easy source of small talk, but Silas didn't trust himself enough to hide the emotions he was sure were plastered across his face. The emotions that had been swirling in his stomach ever since the parade.

There was only one person who Silas wanted to talk to. He grabbed his earbuds off the nightstand and headed downstairs.

"I'm going for a walk," he said.

His parents looked up from the couch.

"Sierra's already asleep, but do you mind keeping an ear out just in case she wakes up?"

"Of course," his mom said. She studied his face, as if her motherly instinct could tell something was off. "Be safe."

Silas tried to hide his smile while he headed to the door. His mom had been telling him to stay safe for as long as he could remember. It bugged him as a kid, but now he could hear the phrase for what it was. Another way to say she loved him.

"I'll be back soon."

Silas wasn't sure how long he'd really be gone. It all depended on if Hope answered his call. He put his earbuds in as soon as he was past the hearing distance of the house. There was no way he wanted his family to hear the call he was about to make.

Hope answered on the second ring, and the words froze on Silas's tongue.

"I'm sorry," he finally said. He blurted out the words. Quick and to the point. Thankfully no one was around to see how he smacked a hand to his forehead.

There was laughter in Hope's voice when she answered. "Oh really? I'm not sure why you should be."

Her words brought him to a halt. "I almost kissed you today. And I don't have the right to do that anymore."

He could still imagine the pressure of her lips on his. Kissing her as a teenager had been easy. It was something he looked forward to every time they were together.

Hope was quiet for so long that Silas began to count heartbeats. She was thinking, and he knew better than to interrupt her thoughts. Her voice had no waver to it when she finally spoke.

"Then I'm sorry, too. I'm sorry we didn't have longer to hang out together. And I'm sorry that I didn't get to give you a real kiss goodbye before you left."

The words sucked the air out of Silas's lungs. "You aren't angry?"

Hope's laughter was a caress down his back. "Should I be? The way I see it, we're adults now. We'd both be willing participants, so why worry?"

She cleared her throat before continuing. "Besides, what's the big deal about a kiss between old friends?"

"You've got a point." The road curved up ahead and Silas followed, walking by a deep field. She was friend-zoning him, which was a safe place to be. He could handle the idea of being friends. "How did the rest of the afternoon go? Did Reid and Millie float home?"

A soft chuckle came through the phone. "They are insufferable. I think they should have gotten engaged months ago, but she wanted to wait. I'm pretty sure they'll be popping out babies before anyone else gets a chance."

Silas wanted to see Hope's face while they talked. He was sure she'd be talking with her hands, waving them excitedly back and forth to make her point. That was one of the things he had loved about her in the past.

"What about your other brothers? Aren't Thomas and Hazel coming up on their first anniversary? You don't think they're planning to start a family any time soon?"

Hope was quiet again, for just a moment. "I don't think so. I tried to ask them about it once, but didn't get far. I don't think they'll be ready to start their family for a while."

"What about Porter and Emily?" As Silas asked the questions, he couldn't help but think of Sierra, sleeping soundly in her bed with a smile across her face. He wondered if he'd ever give her a sibling to play with.

The snort that shot through the phone startled Silas. Hope sounded almost angry. "Bree let me think they were pregnant, hinting about news they had to share."

He could tell where this answer was going. "And let me guess. They're not."

"Nope." Hope's laugh was laced with an edge of frustration. "She isn't pregnant, but another one of her llamas is. One is due to be born soon, and the other won't be here until next year."

"That will be fun, too." Silas wasn't sure how to read the tone in Hope's voice. Why would the birth of a llama make her upset?

"It will, but I was really looking forward to being an aunt. Do you have any idea how spoiled the first grandchild in my family will be?"

Silas could imagine it clearly. "I'm guessing, with all those aunts and uncles, the first child will be pretty loved. But knowing your family, so will each of the babies that follow."

"True." A door banged in the background, and then the sound of crickets came chirping through the phone. Hope had gone outside. She cleared her throat. "How was your family when Sierra was born? Were they supportive?"

Her words caught him off guard. He didn't think she'd want to hear even more about the child who forced the two of them apart. "They weren't very supportive at first. At least, in my opinion they weren't."

"Why not?"

Silas sucked in the clear night air, trying to bring back the emotions from that time. "I was a young, nineteen-year-old boy. I had been hiding so much from my parents. All I could see was their disappointment in me. In what I'd done."

He waited for Hope to agree with him, but she didn't speak. The steady chirping of the crickets through the phone was his only indicator that she was there.

"I'd been encouraged to save intimacy for marriage, but I hadn't cared. Not in the moment. Not that night. And once Zoe was pregnant, there was nothing I could do to hide my actions. In the beginning, I was so angry at myself, I couldn't see past it. I didn't give my parents a chance to support me. I just assumed they were mad."

"I'm sorry." Hope's voice was soft. "That must have been hard."

"Yeah." Silas closed his eyes, realizing that even though he wasn't standing next to Hope, they were both outside, sharing the same night sky. "It took a while for me to realize that both my parents stood behind me, and that they really wanted to get to know Sierra."

The memories that were crowding into Silas's mind weren't comfortable. He had spent the first couple of years jumping from one mistake to the next. There was a lot of anger and tears during that time period. Silas had been constantly worried that Zoe would take Sierra and vanish into the night. He had been stretched to his limits, but he had overcome them to become the dad he was today.

"I still remember the look on my mom's face the first time she got to hold Sierra. The love there was hard to miss. It honestly surprised me, how she could love the small human so much, even with the hurt her situation had brought."

"She sounds like a perfect grandma to me." Hope's voice was soft, like she had been hanging onto his every word. "I haven't seen you in the dad role for long, but from the bits I've seen, Sierra is lucky to have you." Something caught in Hope's throat and she cleared it. Silas wasn't sure if he was imagining the emotion when she spoke again.

"If you're half as good to Sierra as you were to me . . ." She stopped speaking, a small sniff coming through the line. "I can't imagine anyone better to be a dad."

Silas let her compliment wash over him. Most women either pretended like Sierra was a burden or they were overly nice with their words. It felt like they were trying to get close to Sierra so they could get close to him. An agenda. But Hope didn't act that way.

"Thanks."

Silas leaned against a fence post and looked at the sky. "Can you see the moon from where you're standing?"

That soft laughter caressed his heart. "I can."

"Me too." He took a second to gather his thoughts. "I'm glad, even though circumstances are complicated, that I can be close enough to you to share the moon. I hadn't realized how much I needed to see you again."

He could hear her breath hitch in her throat. Another

soft breath. He had to get his words out before she said anything else. She deserved honesty.

"Hope, I don't know what tomorrow will bring, but I do know that the past few days with you have brought me more peace than anything else in my life. The thought of not seeing you tomorrow makes me sad."

"What are you saying?"

Silas ached to see Hope's face. He didn't want to have this conversation through the phone. What he wanted was to be with her. To kiss her for real, not chickening out behind a thin fishing booth curtain. He wanted to press a kiss to her face for every tear he had caused.

He took a deep breath. "I want to see if there's still a chance that you and I could work together. I want to take you out on another date, and hear more about you. I want to see if maybe, deep down, there's still something between us."

"Silas." Her voice held a whisper of longing and his heart raced. "I want that, too. But would it be wise? I mean, we're two completely different people now."

"That's my point. We're not the same people we were in high school. Maybe I have nothing in common with the new version of you, and maybe you can't stand the new version of me, but that wasn't how I felt today at the park."

He could imagine Hope biting the side of her cheek while considering his words. "So you think you might like me a little bit, still?" Her words were filled with laughter. "Because I know I had a great day with you."

"Yeah. I still like you, just a little bit." Silas hooked a

thumb through a loop on his jeans. He was being more honest than he had been in years. Teasing Hope lifted his spirits.

"I guess that's good, because I might like you a little bit, too."

"So what do we do now?" Silas had gotten through the difficult part. Now he was filled with an anxious energy. He was half tempted to jog to Hope's house, just to see her. It had been a long time since any woman made him feel that way.

Hope began to laugh. "I'm not used to hanging out with you in any responsible sort of way. Maybe we should sneak out of our houses and meet under the bleachers at the school."

"Or we could crash a school dance, somewhere." He had always loved dancing with her.

Her laughter filled the air again, curling around Silas like a warm blanket. "I like that we have possibilities."

"Me too." Silas turned down another road, only half paying attention to where his feet were going. "Do you want to go on a picnic with me tomorrow?"

"That would be nice." Hope groaned softly. "Can you hold on a minute?"

"Sure." Silas waited while the sound of the chirping crickets disappeared from Hope's end. He assumed she had gotten another call.

Three minutes later, she wasn't back. Silas held out his phone, which showed him still being connected. He kept walking.

A gnawing worry crept through Silas's stomach when she wasn't back after five minutes. Was she getting bad news?

He was getting ready to hang up the phone when Hope's voice came back. All the laughter was gone. "Are you still there?"

"I am."

"I need to tell you something."

His stomach dropped to the ground. "Are you okay?"

"It was the Ginny Brooks band. They just asked me to go on tour."

Her words sounded like they were coming from the end of a dark tunnel. Silas struggled to keep his breathing even. "When?"

There was a sharp intake of breath on the other end of the phone. "They want me on a plane tomorrow."

CHAPTER 13

Hope's hands were shaking. She should be elated about the call she had just taken, but everything was happening too fast. She didn't want to talk to Silas about it. Not over the phone. This was a conversation that should be happening in person.

She looked up at the sky where stars twinkled. How many times had she looked at the sky, wishing for her life to go the way she wanted it to? It didn't seem right that she was getting one dream at the expense of another.

A snap decision had her turning around and heading back to the house.

"Where are you?" she asked.

"Uh, I'm not really sure. Give me a sec."

Hope grabbed her keys from a hook by the door and headed for her car.

Her car was purring down the road in the general

direction of Silas's house when he reported back. "I'm near the old Rucker house."

That was the abandoned house that they used to think was haunted. She headed down the road towards where Silas walked, determined to make at least one part of the evening go right.

"What time do you leave?" he asked. "Is there time for breakfast together?"

Hope pretended like she couldn't hear the sadness in his voice. If she let herself feel bad, she'd never go. "We head for the airport at ten."

Silas sucked in a breath. "That soon? I mean, I guess Ginny is famous enough, she can get people to show up whenever she wants."

He wouldn't ask her to stay. Hope knew that. And he couldn't go with her. Not while he had a daughter at home to take care of.

"I was their second choice. They'd already been rehearsing with their first choice, but something happened so they reached out to me. I think that's why they want me to come right away."

"How do you feel about that? Being second?"

Hope hadn't been asked that yet. The news was so fresh, she hadn't even told her family. She took a beat to consider her answer so it was honest.

"I don't think I care. I mean, it would have been great to be their first choice, but in the end it wouldn't have mattered if I was twentieth on their list. I'm getting to tour with one of the most popular singers around."

"You're going to be amazing. You might stop talking to all of us lowly people, but you'll be amazing."

A low chuckle came through the phone, and Hope pressed her foot to the gas pedal. She wanted the conversation to stay light until she could see Silas, face to face.

She didn't owe Silas any explanation for why she was leaving but she was grateful for his support. They had almost kissed in the park, and Hope would be lying if she said she hadn't been looking forward to getting to know Silas again. They deserved a real goodbye this time.

Chatting about the ridiculous outfits she was going to have to wear kept the conversation going for another few minutes until Hope pulled onto a dark road. She drove slowly, scanning the sides of the road until she saw Silas, hands in his pockets, walking near a fence.

He looked over his shoulder at her, noticed the car, and moved even further to the side. Hope slowed the car to a stop beside him, rolling down her window.

"Get in," she said.

Silas locked his eyes on her, his mouth in a smirk, until his gaze landed on the arm that rested on the window, still wrapped in a cast.

"Why are you driving?" he asked. He planted his hands on his hips. "Didn't your doctor give you any instructions at all?"

Hope lifted her chin. "He isn't here. Besides, I wanted to talk to you."

Silas held out his phone. "I thought that's what we were doing."

"We were. But I wanted to talk to you in person."

The words hung in the air, waiting for Silas to answer. He walked slowly to the car, resting both hands on the door. As he bent down to study Hope's face, a memory shot through her.

They were in high school, and he had walked her to her car that day. She didn't know what they talked about, or why he didn't get in the car, but she remembered the kiss he gave her, leaning in through the open window. The memory of it sent heat to her cheeks.

Silas straightened up with a shrug. "I don't know. I'm really enjoying my walk."

His words were teasing, but Hope wasn't going to let him go that easily. She pulled off to the side of the road and got out of the car, locking the doors behind her.

Silas tried to smooth his expression when she headed to his side, slipping her hand in his. "Then let me join you."

She lifted her head to his, a challenge dancing in her eyes.

They turned back towards the road, and without missing a beat, Silas lifted her hand to his chest. He gave her a little squeeze before lowering their hands, keeping a tight grip when they turned to look at the old house.

"Do you know if the old balance beam is still by the river?" Silas asked.

Hope scrunched her forehead, trying to remember what her family had told her about the property. "I'm not sure. Do you want to check?"

Silas stopped walking and held a hand to his mouth. "Are you suggesting that we trespass on private property?"

She grinned and tugged him forward. "Of course. It didn't stop us as teens. Why should it be any different now?" The land had been vacant for so long, no one really cared who passed through. A faint trail wound through the grass where hundreds of feet had passed on their way to the river on the other side of the property.

They followed the path, keeping on the trail until they could hear the babble of the river. With a small tug, Silas pulled Hope off the path to head towards their secret spot. Tall stalks of grass brushed against Hope's legs but she didn't mind. Her anticipation rose with each step.

Finally, Silas stopped. Hope stood beside him, waiting for her eyes to adjust to the moonlit night. She looked around their surroundings, surprised by how little had changed over the years.

Trees stretched to the left and right before curving to follow the river bank. The sound of crickets was loud, as was the sound of the rushing water. Hope pressed a hand to her mouth when she caught sight of the old tree, with a low branch that grew sideways towards the other side of the bank.

"I can't believe it's here," she whispered. She was afraid to break the magic of the night by speaking too loudly.

"Do you think it's still safe?" Silas asked. He walked onto the branch, hands held out on either side while he pushed against the bark. He jumped a few times and the tree responded with a slight bounce that made him wobble.

Hope drank in the sight of his smile when he turned back to her, his hand pumping the air.

"I think we're good," he said.

It took less than a minute for them to take off their shoes, leaving them by the side of the river in the tall grass. They walked in single file to the center of the wide branch, where the limb split into two smaller branches that arched to the opposite bank. Hope turned to face Silas.

"Do you need a hand?" His eyes glinted in the moonlight, his words a challenge.

Hope squared her shoulders. She glanced down at her wrist, debating how smart it would be to try to sit down without help.

Silas just laughed and held out his arm, helping her to balance while she sat on the first branch, holding her feet up so they didn't touch the water. He sat on the branch opposite her, his knees touching hers.

Hope exhaled, telling herself that the shivers coursing through her body had everything to do with the river and the warm breeze that wafted past. Not the man sitting across from her.

"Are you ready?" he asked.

Hope nodded, and together they began to count. When they reached three, they plunged their toes down into the icy cold water of the river below.

Hope clamped a hand over her mouth, trying to stifle her shriek. The giggles that came afterwards were hard to stop.

"I forgot how cold this river is," Silas said. He reached

his hands out and rubbed them up and down Hope's arms. "Are you okay?"

She was shivering but his hands were warm.

There were two ways to end this night. The first would be to sit on the branches of the tree and talk like good friends who had been reunited. That option was wise. Hope was leaving in the morning. It was far easier to say goodbye as friends.

The other option was to lean forward, like she had done all those years before and let Silas wrap her in a cocoon of warmth. This was their secret spot. The place where he had held her while they talked about their future plans together. It was also the place she'd visited after he left, whenever she missed him so much that her heart ached.

Silas continued rubbing her arms while he watched her, wisely biding his time until she was ready to speak.

"I want to kiss you goodbye," she finally said. "But I don't think I should."

"Oh, really?" A smirk lifted the edge of his mouth. "And why is that?"

Hope pressed her hand to his knee. She studied the eyes that were flecked with blue, his hair dark as the night.

"Would you believe that I'm afraid?" Hope traced a line back and forth on Silas's knee, not daring to say more.

Silas leaned back and ran a hand through his hair. "Yeah. I believe you because I'm afraid, too. It doesn't make sense to kiss you right now. Especially with you leaving tomorrow. I don't know if my heart can take saying goodbye again. But then, sitting by you like this, it's hard to remember my reasons why I should stay away."

He was saying the right words. The smart words. The words that tore through Hope's defenses, shredding them. She tried to focus on the water racing beneath them, making her toes numb. She willed that water to flow through her veins, cooling the heat in her blood.

This was her Silas sitting in front of her. She knew the curve of his mouth. The weight of his hands. She knew how easy it would be to close the gap between them and let his mouth finish the apology he had been trying to say all week.

Her hand stilled on his knee. "Is it okay if you just wrap your arms around me and hold me tight like you used to?"

The words sounded childish coming out of her mouth, but Hope knew her limits. She couldn't head out on tour with the memory of Silas pressed against her lips.

He shifted onto her branch so he was sitting beside her. Then his arm slid around her waist, pulling her close. Hope closed her eyes and leaned against his side.

The water raced and crashed against the boulders below, but the river inside Hope was still. She didn't know where the path with Silas would lead, but in this moment, she could believe that she was whole. She was leaning against her rock.

Silas didn't speak while he held her. He just slowly stroked her waist, his fingers traveling up and down in a small circle. After a few minutes he leaned down to rest his head against hers.

Hope lifted her hand to stroke his cheek, running her finger across his five o' clock shadow. "I think sitting like this was one of the things I missed the most when you were gone. Spending time together with no real responsibilities."

Silas leaned into her touch. He pressed a kiss to the top of her head. "You have no idea how much I missed days like this, too. I thought about coming back every hour of every day in the beginning. It was so hard to remember that there was a reason I had left."

Hope thought about how it would have felt for him to come back. "As messed up as it sounds, I'm glad you didn't. I think watching you leave again would have torn me apart."

Silas leaned back and Hope instantly missed his warmth. He repositioned his arm so it was draped across her shoulders. "I don't know. Maybe it would have healed both of us faster, to have a real goodbye."

Hope's heart was beating fast. "Maybe." She lifted her face to look at his, shadowed in the moonlight. "What do we do now?"

Silas gave her shoulder a reassuring squeeze. "I'm going to go home, and keep searching for answers to help Sierra. I'm going to tuck the memories of this night into my heart, and whenever I'm missing you, this is what I'm going to pull out."

His lips grazed the top of her head again, and Hope couldn't help but smile.

"You are going to go on tour, and be the best opening

act Ginny Brooks has ever seen. One day, you're going to roll back into town, with all your groupies, and you're going to look me up."

Another kiss. Hope's heart was melting into a pile of goo. "Maybe. The fame might have gone to my head. I'll make you wait in line with the rest of my adoring fans."

Silas laughed, pulling her close. "If I have to wait in line to see you, I'd better get a personalized autograph. Maybe a picture to hang on my wall so I can remember that I knew you before you were famous."

Hope squeezed his knee in the right spot, causing him to jump.

His eyes were gleaming when he caught her hand and pulled it to his chest. "Thank you for tonight. For all our nights, really."

The ache to kiss Silas ran deep through Hope's body. Instead, she let out a sigh. "As much as I'd like to sit here forever, I should head back. I still have to pack."

Silas didn't move. "I want one more minute." He pressed his chin to the top of her head, breathing deeply. "One minute to memorize everything about you and this place. I want to lock this memory into my mind so I'll never forget."

Hope lifted her hand to his cheek a final time. "Me too."

She traced the line of his cheek bones and the angle of his jaw, replacing her old memories with this new one. He sucked in his breath when she gently traced the contour of his lips, his skin warm against her fingers.

Silas waited until her hand was still before he moved, pushing back with a groan.

"You sure about that not kissing thing?"

She tickled his knee again in response and he jerked away before pulling her up with a laugh.

"If I'm supposed to kiss you, our paths will cross again," Hope said. She walked back to her car, hand in hand with Silas, wishing with all her heart that her words would come true.

CHAPTER 14

Silas knew he would miss Hope, but he had no idea how much he would think about her once she was gone. She promised she'd keep in touch, but her schedule had been non-stop busy, with only three weeks to get an opening act ready to match the energy of Ginny Brooks.

The first time she called, he was in the middle of reading a bedtime story to Sierra. He hated sending the call to voicemail, but Sierra, Coco and Simmy were all waiting to be tucked into bed. Fifteen minutes later he was able to call back, but he had missed his window. Hope didn't answer the phone.

The following afternoon he took Sierra and her cousins to splash in the reservoir. One of the trees nearby had fallen in a storm. The branches hung out over the water, and Silas found himself reaching for his phone. He snapped a quick photo and texted it to Hope.

I found a backup tree if ours ever falls.

A minute later she texted back a laughing emoji. **I guess we'll have some new memories to make.**

His sister caught him smiling at his phone. "What are you grinning about?"

Silas showed the picture to Rose, silently praying that Hope wouldn't send another text while he was holding his phone out.

"A tree? What's so funny about that?"

Silas shrugged. "Nothing, really. It just reminds me of one of my old friends."

Rose looked like she wanted to push further, but the girls ran up, shivering, as a cloud blocked the sun. They dried them off and ran to the car, closing the doors right as gigantic rain drops pelted the reservoir.

"Who's ready for ice cream?" Rose asked. The girls cheered and they were off to the next adventure.

Silas spent the rest of the afternoon waiting for Hope to text or call, but his phone was quiet. She was in the middle of finalizing a set list, so Silas told himself she was busy. It didn't stop him from checking his phone every half hour to see if he missed a call from her.

It took a week, but they slowly figured out a schedule for brief calls. It didn't give Silas nearly enough time to hear about Hope's adventures, but it was going to have to be enough.

He was surprised when the first postcard appeared. It was a picture of a dolphin wearing sunglasses. Scrawled across the back was a note.

Hello from sunny Florida. The show opens tomorrow. I wish you were here on the front row to cheer me on. - Hope

The card arrived two days after the concert, but Silas appreciated the thought. He sent her a text.

I wish I could have been there, too. I looked at some reviews online. It sounds like the crowd loved you.

He didn't add that he missed her or that he would have given almost anything to watch her perform. Her reply came through later that evening.

You would have been proud. I managed to walk onto the stage without slipping on anything. No more broken bones for me.

Silas found a GIF of a person slipping on a banana peel and sent it. In return, he got a frowning emoji.

Do you have time to talk tonight? Silas pushed send, even though he could guess what her answer would be.

The reply came back far too quickly. **I'd love to, but I can't. We have a press event tomorrow morning. I need my beauty sleep.**

He tried to stuff down his disappointment.

I'm not sure how to tell you this, but you've already got the beauty thing down.

A string of sleeping emojis came through, followed by a heart. It took Silas a long time to fall asleep that night. He spent an hour staring at the ceiling, wishing he owned a private airplane so he could fly to see her.

Silas was in the family room a few days later, talking to his boss, when his mom brought in another postcard. The front showed the Chicago skyline at night, tall skyscrapers reflecting off the water in shades of yellow and blue. There wasn't a lot of writing on the back, but the words brought a smile to his face.

Looking at the same moon as you. - Hope

Silas slipped the card into a drawer in his desk, right on top of the Florida postcard. Hope had been gone for a month already. During that time, Silas had temporarily moved back in with his parents. Every day brought more color to Sierra's cheeks and more energy to her playing. He couldn't tell why she was healing. No one could. He wasn't in a hurry to take her back to the city and risk her getting sick again.

He never imagined that he'd be the sort of man who had to move back home. Compared to Hope, he knew his life looked boring. She was touring the country while he re-acquainted himself with the town he grew up in.

Silas wondered if Hope was embarrassed to talk to him. The high caliber of people she was surrounded with made him look pale in comparison. He could tell her the best types of trees to plant in an area and how to avoid forest fires. Not how to make millions performing in front of sold out audiences.

When the third postcard came, Silas had to listen to a good natured ribbing from his sister Mia before she'd hand it over. He thought Mia was just being obstinate until he saw the front of the postcard. The letters L, O, V, and E were stacked on each other in a sculpture between two tall buildings. A banner saying Philadelphia, PA draped across the top.

"She loves you," Mia sang, dancing out of the way when Silas swung a kitchen towel at her.

"It's just a cool sculpture," Silas said. He was glad Mia couldn't tell how fast his heart was beating when he flipped the card over to read Hope's message.

They call this the city that loves you back. I'm not sure if that's true, but the crowd tonight was electric. This is my favorite place so far. Maybe we can visit after the tour is over. - Hope

Silas held the card to his chest, taking comfort in the fact that Hope was reaching out. He wanted to hear her voice, but there were dishes to wash and he had promised Sierra a movie night.

The sun was sending up the final, feeble rays when Silas had a minute to get away. He held back a groan when he glanced at his phone. With the time zone differences, Hope was probably already getting ready for bed.

He placed a video call, hoping to get a couple of minutes with her before she fell asleep. As expected, her eyes looked tired when she answered the phone. She yawned, covering her mouth.

"I'm calling too late," Silas said.

"I'm glad you are. I fell asleep on the couch before I even took my boots off."

Hearing Hope's voice instantly lifted the tension from his shoulders. "That's rough. How are you holding up?"

Hope set her phone down so all Silas could see was a swish of her hair and then the ceiling. Two thuds sounded in the background and then she was back. "Much better."

"Because the boots are off? Or is touring getting easier?" Silas was sitting on the front steps where he'd have some privacy.

"Both." Hope laughed. "Touring is way more difficult than I expected, but I also love it way more than I thought I possibly could. I can't explain how it feels to have a stadium erupting into cheers when I walk onto the stage. I know they are coming for Ginny, but they cheer just as loudly for me."

Silas closed his eyes, letting her excitement wash over him. "I'm sure it won't be long before you're booking your own tours. What's the best part?"

Hope hummed softly. "I think the best part is knowing that I actually made it. I've been telling people I wanted to be a singer for as long as I can remember. Now I'm living that dream. It still feels surreal to walk onto the stage through an archway of sparks with a crowd chanting my name." She ran a hand through her hair, pulling at some tangles.

Silas watched her, surprised at the wave of pride that washed over him. "You worked hard to get to where you are. You deserve every good thing that's coming your way."

A smile lit her face. "Thanks. I know plenty of other people who have worked just as hard as me. They aren't getting these same opportunities. I feel really blessed."

"I get that." Silas had known Hope would be popular. She sang like an angel, and she was gorgeous and genuine. People would gravitate to that. He pushed his jealousy to the side at the thought of who would become part of her life next.

"What's the hardest part?"

Silas watched as Hope's face fell. She lifted her gray eyes to study his, staring through the phone. "I wasn't expecting to be so homesick." Her smile was gone now, and Silas ached to stretch his hand through the phone to wipe away the tears beading in her eyes.

"You miss the city?"

The corner of Hope's mouth twitched, but she didn't smile. "I miss the city, and my friends there. I miss my own bed, and knowing where I'll be each day." She rubbed her cheek, swiping away at the single tear that had started to fall.

Silas ached to pull her close. She was two thousand miles away from him, but the video call made it feel like she could be just around the corner.

"I miss the country, too. They have been spoiling me on this tour. We have the best catering in the area, but I'm already tired of the food. I really want one of my mom's home cooked meals."

"I get that." One of the perks of being home was eating his mom's meals.

Hope sniffed, and then her face softened. "Mostly, I miss being surrounded by people who know me and love me. It's fun to feel adored, but I want someone to call me out on my crap every now and then."

Silas laughed. "I'll happily insult you any day you'd like." He propped his elbows up on his knees, studying Hope's face.

He expected her to look tired because he had just

woken her up. What he didn't expect to see were the dark circles under her eyes.

"Thanks." Hope had been leaning against the couch cushions but she jolted up. "Oh my gosh. I totally forgot. You had an appointment for Sierra this week. How did it go? Is her stomach doing okay?"

Silas nodded. "The doctor was thrilled with her progress. She still has bad days, but she's definitely improving. My mom says it's the country air, and all the sunshine. I'm happy, but don't trust it. What if she gets worse again?"

Hope let out a huff of air. "Thanks for the reality check. I'm over here complaining about not wanting more delicious catering while you're dealing with real life problems."

"It's okay. It's part of being a parent."

Hope nodded. "I'm glad she's doing so much better. Do you think you'll head to the city again?"

Silas picked at a piece of peeling paint on the railing. "I don't know what to do. I never thought I'd be living with my parents at this age, but so far, it seems like the best solution for Sierra. I'm trying to take it one week at a time."

Hope leaned her head back, covering her face with a hand. "I can't believe I dumped all my silly trials on you."

"Why?" Silas ran a hand through his hair. "I want to know your real life. I don't only want to hear about all the happy things that are happening."

Hope's smile pierced his heart. "So you want to hear me fuss about the chicken alfredo pasta I had for lunch?"

"First of all, you should have shared some with me.

That's my favorite. And second of all, yes. If that is what's bothering you, I want to hear about it."

The smile she gave him was soft. "I didn't finish telling you about all the things I missed."

"Right. What else do you miss?" Silas ran his fingers back and forth across the top step, feeling the rough grain of wood beneath his hand. He watched Hope's face.

She cleared her throat. "I miss you, Silas. I feel like we were standing at a precipice, looking down on a world filled with possibilities, and then I walked away."

"Like I did." There was no judgment in Hope's words, but Silas felt a pang of resentment. This was the second time circumstances had pulled them apart.

"No, not like you did. I mean, at least we were able to talk about it before I left. But we didn't have enough time." She stifled another yawn.

Silas watched as she rubbed her hand across her face. He needed to let Hope get some sleep, but he didn't want her to go while she was sad.

"It wasn't enough?" He grinned at Hope. "So what I'm hearing is that you are wishing you kissed me goodbye when we were sitting at the river."

Hope snorted, her mouth dropping open. "I didn't say that."

"But it's true."

The corner of Hope's mouth twitched up again, hiding a smile. "Yeah. It's true."

"How about this?" Silas's voice was soft when he spoke.

"How about you finish this tour of yours, and then you look me up. We'll see about that kiss. Deal?"

"Deal." Hope's smile was real when she said goodbye.

Silas shifted over so his back was against the railing. He looked at the sky, sending a quick prayer that Hope would be able to enjoy the wild path she was on. Very few people got to follow their biggest dreams. As much as he missed her, he wouldn't want her to be anywhere else.

He pulled himself off the porch and headed into the house, a plan starting to form. Hope was going to be gone for a couple more months, but that didn't mean he couldn't see her.

Silas tapped his fingers against the desk while he waited for his computer to reboot. He had some concert tickets to buy.

CHAPTER 15

Hope stepped out of the hotel lobby, holding a hand to her eyes to block the bright sun. She'd been in Texas for a week, but this was the first time she'd stepped outside other than her brief trip to the doctor.

She was on the fifth week of touring, and her body was feeling it. It didn't seem to matter how much vitamin C she took, or how healthy she ate. She was fighting a cold, and there was no way to get around that.

The doctor had sent her home with strict orders to not talk, which was mostly easy to follow while cooped up in a hotel suite. She sincerely hoped that the four days of rest had been long enough for her voice to bounce back.

Hope was heading towards the car when she heard someone calling her name. She looked across the parking lot to where a tall man was waving his hand wildly in the air.

"Hold on a second," she said to the driver. All thoughts of taking it easy were gone as she ran past rows of cars.

Seconds later she was being swung in a giant circle, her body being crushed by the arms of her best friend. "Monroe," she said, trying not to cry. "What are you doing here?"

He lowered her to the ground with a smile. "You didn't think I'd miss your entire tour, did you?"

Hope shook her head. "I guess not, but you hate Texas. I never thought I'd see you here."

Monroe bumped against her hip. "I don't hate Texas. I just hate the heat."

"Good point." Hope had been so feverish, she hadn't paid much attention to the sweltering weather. "Are you going to watch the show tonight?"

"Yep. I'll be in the front row."

"But how? Those tickets have been sold out since Ginny announced her tour."

Monroe shrugged. "I bought them the minute they went live. I had a pretty good feeling you'd be finding yourself on the stage."

Tears filled her eyes. She was reminded, once again, of how incredible her support group was. "What if they hadn't picked me? I mean, they didn't, at first."

He draped an arm across her shoulder. "I figured I could sell them to someone else. Besides, my gamble paid off."

Hope wrapped her arm around Monroe's waist. "I can't believe you're actually here. Do you want to come to the venue with me?"

Monroe grinned. "Am I allowed to? I'd love that."

Hope nodded. "If you're lucky, maybe I'll introduce you to Ginny."

At her words, Monroe's face fell. "You know I didn't come here for that, right? I'd be cheering for you if you were opening for a local school."

She opened the door and climbed into the car. "I know, but you're right. There are some perks to touring with a famous singer. I want to show all of them to you."

The driver leaned back to confirm their destination. Monroe looked confused as they pulled up in front of a local convenience store.

"Did you need snacks?" he asked.

"Nope." Hope headed for a spinning rack near the front of the store. She flipped through the post cards, trying to find the perfect one for Silas.

"Postcards?" Monroe asked. "Do people even send those things anymore?"

Hope pulled out one that had horses thundering across the bottom. It wasn't as silly as some of the other ones, but it made her think of home.

"I'm not sure about other people, but I do. Besides, given the number of postcards on display, I'd say they are still popular."

Monroe began to flip through the stacks with Hope. He held out a picture of a cactus wearing a cowboy hat, but Hope shook her head.

"Who is this for, anyway?" Monroe asked as they headed to the register to pay.

"Silas." Hope plunked down a couple of dollars and then asked to borrow a pen. She wrote his address in a box on the back.

Monroe's stare was filled with doubt as she began to write her message.

This postcard reminds me of home. It makes me happy to know you are staying near the ranch. Take Sierra to say hi to my horses.

She paused, feeling suddenly self-conscious. No matter what she wrote, Monroe was going to have questions. She hadn't filled him in on her relationship status because she wasn't quite sure what it was.

I miss you. - Hope

Monroe's eyebrows rose when she signed her name and stuck on a flower stamp. He didn't say anything as they walked out of the store. Hope slid the postcard into the large blue mailbox near the door.

"What?" she finally asked.

"Isn't this the guy who broke your heart in high school?" The words were heavy with judgment.

She waved down the driver, grateful for the brief pause so she could gather her thoughts.

"Yes. That was Silas. But he's not the same guy anymore."

Monroe folded his arms across his chest. "Oh really? I think we all know that people don't change much. What makes you think he has?"

To an outside observer, Monroe's words sounded harsh. Hope knew where he was coming from, though.

"We were able to have some good talks when I was home. I forgave him."

"I see." Monroe's arms didn't relax. "What if he hurts you again? He didn't seem to have a problem with it when you guys were younger."

Hope understood why Monroe would think that way. She wasn't sure how to sum up the conversations she had had with Silas. He left because of Sierra, but that wasn't her story to tell. She ran a hand through her hair before facing Monroe.

"I guess that's always a risk. He could tear out my heart completely, and I'd be shattered. But I don't think he will. I'm being more careful this time."

"So you're not falling head over heels in love with the guy who ruined your life?"

"No." Hope paused. "Maybe. I'm not sure how I feel about him yet. All I know is that he makes me happy. Mending our relationship has been good for me."

Monroe shrugged, his posture finally relaxing. "I hope it works out."

"I do too." Hope rested her head against the window, feeling like she had just run a marathon. It was time to change the subject. "That's enough about me. Tell me about Felicity."

The remainder of the drive to the events center went far too fast. It felt like one minute, Hope was asking Monroe about his newest girlfriend, and the next, they were pulling in front of a large stadium.

A flicker of excitement ran through Hope's body at the

sight. She hoped she never lost that burst of excitement, no matter how many stadiums she played.

"Thanks for the ride, Cole," she said. She climbed out of the car and headed to the security guard waiting by the back entrance.

He looked at Monroe with a raised eyebrow.

"Hi Brody. This is my friend, Monroe."

Brody gave a brief nod.

"Monroe, this is Brody. He keeps things safe for us."

"It's nice to meet you," Monroe said. He held out his hand, but Brody folded his arms across his chest.

"I'm going to need you to do a couple of things before I can let you back with Hope."

Brody ordered Monroe to spin in a slow circle, which Monroe did.

Hope covered her smile when Brody instructed Monroe to balance on one foot, and then the other.

"Why am I doing this?" Monroe asked.

"Just standard protocol, Sir," Brody replied. "Now touch your elbow to your knee."

Hope busted up laughing. "I'm sorry, Monroe. Brody likes to give all our guests a hard time." She had heard about Brody's teasing nature, but hadn't seen it in person, yet.

Brody held out a hand to Monroe. "You're friends with one of the good ones. Have a great show, Hope."

"Thanks, Brody."

Monroe opened and closed his mouth a few times before rubbing a hand over his head. He followed Hope down a long hallway. "I was so confused."

"We all spend so much time together, they've become like family. There's a lot of practical jokes here."

Hope let Monroe follow her through all her prep, from the mic check to the makeup chair. She felt a lightness having him by her side. By the time the show was supposed to start, Hope was ready. She snapped a quick selfie before heading onto the stage, which she texted to Silas.

Week five. Wish me luck!

Then she was running through the archway that shot sparks into the air, and heading for the middle of the stage.

* * *

HOPE WAS ONLY HALF surprised to see an article about her and her new mystery man when she turned on her phone the next morning. Reporters had been following the tour, posting about everything from what Ginny ate for dinner to the way they dressed. So far, Hope had been able to stay out of the spotlight.

The pictures of her and Monroe definitely fit the article. She was standing by his side, his arm loosely draped across her shoulders while he leaned down to whisper in her ear. It wasn't surprising the media would blow it out of proportion. They couldn't know that he was leaning down to ask her a question because the music was so loud.

She had been planning to meet Monroe for breakfast before he had to fly home. That no longer sounded appealing. Hope wasn't sure how many people were camped outside the hotel, hoping to catch a sight of someone famous. Ginny was the main draw, but Hope was getting more and more recognition.

It was time to change plans. Monroe knocked on the door to her hotel suite an hour later, holding out a bag of bagels and a fruit smoothie.

"I guess we're dating now?" he asked, a smirk lifting the corner of his mouth. "I'm not sure how Felicity will take the news."

He laughed as he dropped into a chair, setting the bagels on the table in the small sitting area.

Hope groaned. "It's a good thing you're heading back to Utah tonight so you guys can talk. Did you warn her about the article?"

"Not yet. I'm not too worried, though. They only caught the side of my face. You're the one I'm worried about. Have you talked to Silas yet?"

Hope's stomach was tied in knots. "I'm not sure what to say. I mean, we aren't actually dating, so it feels strange to call him up. Do I ask him if he's seen the news?"

"That seems like a good place to start to me." Monroe propped his feet up on the chair opposite him.

"I can see how that conversation would go." Hope held her hand to her cheek like a phone. "Hey Silas. I don't know if you care, but there's rumors that I'm dating someone, even though I'm not. That's just my friend Monroe."

"Smooth start." Monroe was laughing.

"Yeah, so I'm not interested in him because I can't stop

thinking about you. So, uh, maybe ignore the rumors you read?"

She flopped onto the bed with a hand over her face. "I sound like a complete lunatic."

"Or you could try being honest with the guy." Monroe gestured to an empty chair.

Hope walked to the table and tore off a bite of her bagel. "It's hard to be honest when your relationship is kind of in limbo. I don't know what to do."

Monroe gave her arm a gentle squeeze. "You could wait until he brings it up."

That felt like avoiding the situation, but Hope didn't have a lot of options. "I'm worried he'll be too polite to do it, and then we'll have another secret between us. We are trying to be more open."

"Sorry, Sunshine. You're in a tough situation."

She was surprised at the anger she felt towards the paparazzi. They were trying to do their job, but it didn't seem fair to be ruining someone's reputation while they did it. Then again, at least they weren't stalking Sierra and Silas. Hope would gladly have them think she was dating Monroe if it kept the other two safe.

Monroe had to leave shortly after breakfast. Hope gave him a bear hug, thanking him for coming to surprise her. She watched his car pull away until she couldn't see the lights any more. Then she slumped down at the table.

Her body felt weary, and now her heart ached, too. Five weeks was a long time to go without seeing loved ones. She pulled out her phone and turned it over in her hands.

Silas was probably awake by now, but Hope still hesitated to call. She didn't want to ruin their new relationship with a stupid rumor. After a minute, she shook her head from side to side, letting the tension go before she pushed the button to video call him.

Silas answered on the third ring. "Hi Hope. Is everything okay?" His voice was deeper than normal, and Hope realized he had probably been asleep. He was sitting up in his bed, hair sticking out in all directions.

"It's okay. Did I wake you up?"

He gave a wide yawn, covering his mouth. "Not really. I've been awake for the past half hour, but I haven't gotten out of bed yet."

"Sorry." Hope trailed a hand through her hair. "I can call later."

"No. It's okay." He yawned again and rubbed his eyes. "I wanted to talk to you anyway. How did the show go last night?"

The memory of the crowd came flooding back. "It was our biggest crowd since opening night. The audience was electric."

Silas smiled. "And how did your boyfriend like the show?"

He asked the question casually, but Hope's heart stopped. She wasn't sure where to begin, but Silas deserved an explanation. She prayed he'd understand.

CHAPTER 16

Hope went so still, Silas began to worry. He thought he was being funny, but the hitch in Hope's breath told him a different story.

"It's. I'm not. That was Monroe." Her eyes were wide with concern.

Silas was laughing now. "I know, Hope. I recognized his wavy hair."

She smacked her forehead. "You didn't believe the article?"

"Given that the source was EZ Gossip, I figured it probably wasn't true. Besides, I know you."

Hope began to laugh nervously. "I wasn't sure what to say, or if I should say anything at all. I mean, we aren't exactly dating."

"But we're not, *not* dating either." There had to be a better way to define things. Silas rubbed his stubble. "What do you tell people when they ask if you're single?"

He was being direct. The last time he hadn't been honest with his feelings, he had lost out on a future with Hope. Now that she was back in the picture, he wanted to be sure he didn't mess things up again.

She shrugged, turning her body so her face was in the sunlight. "So far, I've been telling them no comment. I don't think it's anyone's business who I do or don't date."

"I see." He wished he was having the conversation with her by his side. He wanted to trail his hand up and down her arms while they talked.

"What about you?" Hope's gray eyes pierced him. "What do you say when people ask you if you're dating anyone?"

Silas was surprised by the question. "No one has asked me that, yet. I think I'd tell them that there is a woman I am kind of crazy about. And I'd tell them we were still figuring things out ourselves."

"That's a pretty good answer." Hope's smile melted his heart. "Maybe I'll steal it, and tell them there's a man I look forward to talking to every day. The problem is that I don't want the paparazzi bothering you or Sierra."

Silas sucked in a breath. "Thanks. I could handle some press, but the idea of someone following Sierra makes me sick."

"Exactly." Hope's lips pulled up into a lopsided grin. Her eyes held a sparkle that Silas remembered from when they were teens. It was a look that usually came before she got into mischief.

"I know that look," he said. "What are you planning to do?"

Hope shook her head. "It's probably a really bad idea. Especially since the press is suddenly more interested in me, but what if I—". Her words were cut off when a loud rap sounded on her door.

"Hold on a sec," she said, dropping the phone so all Silas could see was the ceiling.

Silas could hear mumbling voices in the background. Hope's cheeks were flushed when she picked up the phone again.

"Sorry about that. I've got to run. We're visiting a children's hospital in an hour and I have to get ready."

There was a pit in Silas's stomach as he said goodbye. He looked forward to every conversation with Hope. She was busy, and he had work to do, but he always felt sad when they had to hang up.

"They're going to love you," he said. "I'll talk to you soon."

Silas sat in bed for a few minutes after Hope hung up the phone. Then he pulled his legs to the edge of the bed with a groan. If Hope was going to be a responsible grown up, he could be, too. He stood in the shower, shifting his thoughts from the beautiful woman he was chatting with to the responsibilities of the day, trying to get his mind set on work.

Before long, he was on a conference call with his team, trying to figure out a way to route traffic around a damaged road near one of the more popular camping sites so they could repair it. They would have to turn it into a one way road while the crew worked, which always made people upset. Silas could already hear the complaints of the campers, but there really wasn't anything else to do unless they shut down the campground entirely.

Most of the time, life didn't come with an easy solution to every problem. If it did, he'd be touring with Hope, letting the paparazzi weave whatever stories they liked about their relationship. They would leave Sierra out of it, and everyone would be safe.

It was a good dream, but it wasn't founded in reality. If people started prying into his life, they'd pull up stories of Sierra's birth mom. He would do anything to protect his daughter from having her past drudged up. He was giving her a good life, and that was all they needed to focus on. Even if it meant keeping his growing relationship with Hope a secret.

POSTCARDS FROM TEXAS and Washington joined Silas's pile. He looked forward to getting one each week. They helped him to stay connected to Hope while she traveled the states. He didn't tell her that when she went to Denver, he'd be there in the crowd, cheering her on. It was going to be fun to surprise her.

He video chatted with Hope almost every night. He never knew which version of Hope he'd get. On days off from touring, she wore a simple t-shirt or sweater, with her hair pulled back. Sometimes she was in exercise clothes, but she was almost always casual. The days she toured were a different story.

Some nights she chatted with him on her limo ride back to the hotel. Every speck of her face was covered in makeup and her hair cascaded in curls. Silas knew she loved getting dressed up. It was easy to understand why the internet was blowing up with pictures of her performing. She was stunning.

His favorite nights were the ones where she answered the phone, her hair still damp from the shower. Dark strands of hair would stick to her temples, but her eyes were always bright. He liked seeing her with no makeup on, totally relaxed. This version of Hope felt like it was just for him.

The phone call with Hope the evening before had been short. She was catching an airplane to Las Vegas, where she'd be playing to her biggest audience yet. It hurt Silas to think that she was just a state away, but he couldn't see her. He reminded himself that she'd be singing in Denver in three weeks.

Silas was pulling on a black t-shirt when Sierra came running into the room. "Daddy, Daddy. It's time for our class."

"What is Miss Bree going to show you today?"

He already knew the answer. Every week Bree taught the girls about a new animal. The girls hadn't stopped telling everyone that they were playing with the horses again this week.

"The horses!" She grabbed for his hand, pulling him towards the door. "Come on. We can't be late."

Rose met him by the front door, her face pale. "Thanks for driving them," she said. "I know it was supposed to be my turn."

"You look awful. Get some rest." Silas said. "I'm glad to do it."

Silas loaded Sierra and his nieces into the car. Their chatter from the back seat brought reassurance to Silas's mind. His daughter was thriving in the country.

He pulled onto the ranch, bracing his heart for the memories of Hope that always blasted him when he pulled into the driveway. This time, they drove right past the house to the field. Chatter from the girls trailed off when Silas stopped the car. Bree was nowhere to be seen. She was usually waiting to greet them.

Silas glanced at the clock on the dashboard. They were right on time.

"Are we going to see the horses today, Uncle Silas?" Lacy asked.

"I hope so." Silas peered out the window. "I'm not sure where your teacher is."

Sierra unbuckled her seatbelt to kneel on top of her seat. "She's probably in the barn," Sierra said, sitting back down.

Silas nodded. He didn't usually stay with the girls, but he wasn't going to leave them in a field with no supervision. "Should we check it out?"

At that moment, Bree emerged from the barn, an apologetic smile on her face. "Sorry about that," she called to the group as they climbed out of the car.

Silas followed the girls across the field until they came to a stop in front of Bree.

"Hi girls," she said. "Who is ready to see the horses?" She straightened up while the girls cheered.

"Have fun, Sierra." Silas knelt on the ground to hug his daughter. "Have fun, Lacy and Chrissy. I'll see you guys in a little while." He was turning to leave when Bree caught his arm.

"I just realized I left the brushes behind. Can you grab them for me before you go?"

"Sure." Silas changed his course, heading towards the barn. He was getting used to the smell of the ranch, and the way small pieces of straw seemed to stick to every surface.

The front part of the barn was well lit from the sunlight streaming through the door. Silas glanced at the shelves, but there were no brushes. Maybe she left them by the stalls. He headed deeper into the barn, checking each stall as he went.

He was nearing the final stall when a woman called out to him.

"Looking for these?" she asked.

Silas spun around, his pulse jumping. Hope stood in front of him, holding two large brushes in her hands.

It took one heartbeat for Silas's brain to register that he was actually seeing Hope and not a mirage. The next heartbeat, he was pressing her to his chest in a hug. He leaned down to kiss the top of her forehead.

"You're here," he said. He held her back to study her face, trailing a finger down her cheek. "Why are you here?"

Hope grinned up at him. "I'm homesick. We play in Vegas this week. It's too close to not catch a quick flight home."

"I agree." Silas studied her face, noticing the dark circles under her eyes. He traced them softly. "How are you holding up?"

Hope glanced at the brushes in her hand. "Bree really did need these. Let's give them to her, and then I want to show you something. We can talk there."

Silas followed Hope out the door, not quite believing she was really in front of him. He pressed his hand to the small of her back while they walked across the field.

Bree's face lit up when they approached. "Did she surprise you?"

"You were in on it?" Silas asked.

"It was my idea for Hope to hide in the stable," Bree said.

Hope handed her sister the brushes and waved to the girls. "Have fun with the horses."

Silas drank in the sight of her. He knew he had missed her, but having her in front of him pressed that point home. He didn't care what she had planned, as long as they could spend the time together.

Hope led him to the other end of the field, squeezing between the rungs of a fence. Silas followed after her, bending low while he clambered to the other side.

"Where are we going?" he asked.

"You'll see." Hope led him to a small path that wound between the trees. "We're almost there."

A small clearing opened at the end of the trees. Silas followed Hope to the end, taking her hand when she reached back for him. She pulled him off the path, stepping to a large outcropping of rocks.

"Look at the view," she said, her hand still entwined with his.

Fields stretched out as far as the eye could see, the golds and greens dotted with specks of black and brown. Silas sucked in his breath.

"It's beautiful." He slid his hand to Hope's waist, pulling her close. "Do you miss living at the ranch? I know it was a huge part of your life growing up."

A gust of wind whipped by, blowing Hope's hair into her face. She pushed it to the side. "Yes and no. I don't miss the hard work or the late hours. I do miss all my animals though. And I miss the feeling of working side by side with my family. We got a lot closer when my dad died."

Silas leaned his head against hers. Hope had been a junior when he passed. Silas hadn't even met her yet, but the entire community was rocked by the death. The rodeo came with mild injuries all the time, but it was rare for someone to lose their life. That happened to people in other places. Not to someone the community knew and loved.

He hadn't been in Hope's life that first year, when Hope and her family were trying to adjust to a world without their favorite person in it. By the time he met Hope, she acted normal around her friends. He didn't catch her crying until they had been dating for a month.

"I wish I had been able to support you better, back then. I didn't know what to say or what to do."

Hope leaned her head against his side. Silas turned so he could hug her properly, folding her into his embrace. Her head rested against his heart.

"I felt like I was in the middle of the ocean, constantly being buffeted back and forth. You were someone I could let my guard down with, and actually grieve. Short of bringing my dad back, there wasn't really anything else you could have done."

I could have stayed, Silas thought, but he didn't say it. Hope had forgiven him, and he needed to move on. There was no sense wasting their time together with more apologies. He rubbed a circle on her back before tangling his fingers through her hair.

"You know you're a pretty incredible person, right?" Silas pressed his cheek to the top of her head.

"You're not so bad yourself." Hope let out a small sigh before she straightened up, stepping out of his embrace.

Silas wanted to protest, but then she grabbed his hand and was pulling him towards an almost invisible path through the weeds.

"Let's go," she said.

"Should I be worried?" Silas asked.

Hope's bright laughter surrounded him. "Not if you trust me."

CHAPTER 17

Tall stalks of grass smacked against Hope's legs as she waded through, following a narrow path that only she could see. The pressure of Silas's hand in hers was hot in the sun, but she wasn't interested in letting go. She was enjoying the feeling of him beside her.

She led him through knee-high stalks of grass until they were standing near the bottom of a small hill, dotted with trees.

"Do you remember this place?" Hope asked.

Silas's brow wrinkled. "I don't think so. Should I?"

"You'll see."

Hope squeezed his hand, gently pulling him past the first row of trees towards a small clearing. They headed to a tall oak tree that stood on the crown of the hill. Thick branches stretched from side to side, with an old platform nestled near the base.

Silas shook his head, his eyes lighting with recognition. "Did you guys actually finish the tree house?"

"Not quite." Hope walked around the tree, stopping when they came to a makeshift ladder of boards nailed into the trunk of the tree.

"Are we going up?" Silas asked.

Hope placed her foot on the bottom rung. "Why not?" She pressed on the board a few times before trusting it with her weight. "It feels sturdy enough."

Silas cupped his hands around her hips, the pressure sending heat through her body.

"Do you think I can't climb a tree?" Hope teased.

"All I know is that I remember carrying wood for this project. I don't know who nailed these boards in, but I'm not sure I trust them to still be strong."

"It was Porter, but I won't tell him you are questioning his construction skills. He'd be offended." Hope reached for the next rung, a wave of nostalgia washing over her. The siblings had started with grand goals for a treehouse, but interest waned after the platform was completed. Her older brothers had gone off to college and the project was forgotten.

Hope was turning to smile at Silas when her boot slipped. The hands that had been loosely clamped around her waist tightened, and she turned to see Silas, the expression in his eyes guarded as he lowered her to the ground.

"What were you saying about the ladder being safe?" he asked. His tone was light, but his hands were shaking against her jeans.

Hope turned to face him, her breath hitching when she realized that he wasn't letting go, even though she was safely on the ground.

There wasn't a lot of space between them. Silas hooked his fingers in her belt loops and pulled her close, closing the gap between them.

"I thought it would be fine," she said. Her voice quavered. After weeks of being apart, she was questioning her wisdom in returning home for the surprise visit. How was she going to be able to handle leaving again? Every touch sent a wave of longing through her.

"Do you want to try again?" Silas asked.

Hope nodded. This time, she carefully tested each foothold before putting her weight on it. She squeezed her body through the narrow opening and walked to the edge of the platform. A second later Silas stood beside her, the heat of his body warm beside her.

He lifted his hand, pulling a leaf from her hair before tucking it behind her ear. Then he lowered his hands to her waist. Hope rested her hands on his, waiting for him to make another move. She wanted to kiss Silas. Her lips tingled at the thought of it, but it wasn't her decision to make. Not entirely. Not when she was the one who was going to be leaving.

Hope traced lines on the back of his hands. "You asked me if there was a way to describe our relationship. At the time, I didn't have a good answer."

Her heart was racing, the pulse drumming in her ears so loudly, she was sure it echoed through the clearing.

Silas's voice was low when he answered her. "You have an answer now?"

Hope looked into the eyes of the man she had never stopped caring about. The years had broken them apart, and changed important parts of each of them, but he had always held her heart. She didn't want to give it to anyone else.

"I want to be your girlfriend," she said. It felt like she was in grade school, passing him a note. "I want to know that if anyone asked, I could tell them about you. That you make me happy. That you understand me in a way no one else can."

She ran her hand up his arm until it was resting on his bicep. "I want to shout the way I feel to the crowds I perform for. But I won't. Because more than the desire to share you with the world, I want to protect you and Sierra. I know she'll be an important part of this relationship, if you're willing to give me a chance."

"You want to date me?" His eyes were in shadow, impossible to read.

"If you'd let me." Hope stood still, not trusting her voice to say more.

His hands were moving from her waist now, sliding up her back to her shoulders. "I think I could get used to that."

Hope placed a hand over his heart. "Do you remember what I said, when we were sitting on our branch? About not wanting to kiss you goodbye?"

"I do." His mouth twitched into a lopsided grin.

"Well." She licked her lips, her mouth suddenly dry. "Do you think that was the right choice?"

Silas caressed her cheek, his hand rough against her skin. He traced a slow line down the side of her jaw to the hollow of her throat, where her pulse beat rapidly against his skin. Hope could try to hide how she felt, but her body was betraying her with every thump of her heartbeat against her chest.

There was fire in Silas's eyes as he slid his hand to the side of her neck, curling a lock of her hair around his finger. "I didn't like the decision back then, but I understood it."

"And now?" She was breathless with anticipation as she leaned into his touch.

"And now, I think I'm done being wise."

With that, Silas closed the gap between them. The pressure of his lips on her mouth was light, giving her space to pull away, but that wasn't what Hope wanted. She grabbed the front of his shirt, standing on her tiptoes while she pulled him closer.

He responded with a moan, deepening the kiss so Hope could feel the hunger in his touch. His strong, tender hands cupped the back of her neck while his fingers tangled in her hair.

Heat exploded from Hope like a wave, her heart beating so wildly that she gasped.

Silas broke the kiss, stepping back with concerned eyes. "Are you okay?" He dropped his hands, increasing the distance between them.

"I forgot how it felt," she said. "How it felt to kiss you. I replayed our last kiss over and over in my mind, trying to remember every detail because I hadn't known it would be our last. In my mind I built it up to something epic. Something that no one would ever be able to match."

Silas's mouth twitched, his eyes hungry. "And now?"

"And now I'm realizing that my memory is very, very flawed."

She watched Silas's eyes widen and then he folded his arms across his chest. "Are you saying I'm a bad kisser?" His tone was light, but his eyes held concern.

"I'm saying that if I had remembered our kisses feeling the way this one did, I'd have searched the ends of the earth to find you. I wouldn't have let you go."

The corner of his mouth twitched, and then he was kissing her again, pressing his lips to the hollow of her throat before he moved his way to her mouth. Every kiss was an apology, and also a promise.

Hope's eyes closed and she slid her hands over the curves of his shoulders, tracing the contours of his muscles.

She was grateful for the cool breeze that danced through the trees when they broke apart. There was heat in her cheeks and the taste of Silas on her lips.

"It's probably a good thing this platform wasn't finished when we were teens." Silas slid a hand across his brow. "I think it would have been one of my favorite places to kiss you. Your mom might have gotten suspicious if we kept sneaking off."

Hope winked at Silas. "I remember a few places we snuck off to. Do I need to refresh your memory?"

"You probably should." His voice was husky as he smoothed down the back of her hair. "How long are you here?"

"Two days." Hope slid her arm around Silas's waist and curled into his embrace. "And I'm going to make sure we can find every one of those places before I head back out."

Silas's chest shook with laughter. "I'm in." A hunger filled his eyes. "But first, I think we'd better finish our study of this place."

Hope laughed when he sat on the platform, pulling her down to the wood beside him. His lips were gentle when he kissed her this time, each kiss knitting together a piece of her heart that had been broken.

THE TIME with Silas passed too quickly. Before Hope knew it, she was heading back up the trail with him. They ducked through the rungs of the fence and walked to where Sierra and her cousins were waiting to be picked up.

Hope watched as Sierra ran into her dad's arms, talking so fast, it was hard to follow the words. "Bree let us take care of the horses today. There was a brown horse and a white one and one that had spots. I can't remember his name but he was really nice and he let me brush his mane."

All of Silas's attention was focused on Sierra, but he met Hope's eyes when he pulled his daughter in for a hug. The love for Sierra was evident, but the look he gave Hope told her that there could be room for both of them.

She thought about the ease she had when she was with Silas. Until that moment, she hadn't thought a lot about how Sierra would fit into her future. Sierra was an integral part of Silas's life. Now Hope's heart beat faster watching the young girl.

It was one thing to know that Silas and Sierra were a package deal. Logically, that made sense to Hope's mind. Now she was starting to realize what being with Silas would mean for her future. She wouldn't be just a girlfriend. She'd be a woman in Sierra's life as well. A mentor. A friend.

She watched Silas stand and reach for Sierra's hand, and a vision of the future stretched out before Hope's eyes. Walks with the three of them together, her holding Sierra's other hand. Silas standing beside Hope while Sierra ran through the fields. Tucking Sierra into bed before Silas and Hope headed to their own room.

It was the future Silas deserved. He needed a companion and not just a woman to date. Eventually, the relationship would progress to the point that Silas would be wanting to make his girlfriend a part of his life.

A wave of doubt crashed over Hope. She wasn't in any sort of position to be a mom. She knew she was jumping ahead a number of steps, but wasn't that the smart thing to do? How could she even think about a relationship with Silas when she was following her own hopes and dreams?

Hope walked with the group back to the car, standing

out of the way while Silas buckled Sierra and her cousins into their booster seats. As soon as the door shut with a click, Silas reached for her hand. He pulled her around to the back of the car, out of sight of the girls. Leaning down, he kissed her softly.

"Thank you for today," he whispered. He kissed her cheek a final time before heading to his door.

Hope waved at the car until it was out of sight, her heart bursting with joy.

Bree let out a loud whoop. "Do you want to tell me where you two snuck off to?"

Hope wrapped her arm around her sister's shoulders. "We went for a walk. How was your lesson?"

Bree bumped her side, and Hope laughed. She couldn't exactly hide the kiss from Bree, since she had been standing right there.

"I think I have a boyfriend now, but I'm not sure what that means."

Bree raised an eyebrow. "Last I checked, being boyfriend and girlfriend is pretty straightforward. You like him. He likes you. It's simple."

"On paper, yes. But what about when there's a child involved?"

Bree's expression softened. "I wasn't thinking about that."

"I'm leaving in two days. I want to spend every minute of that time with Silas, but I know Sierra will be there, too. I can't get to know her and then ditch her like her mom did before she died."

Bree took her time answering. "Do you really think going on tour is the same as skipping out on her? Because in my book, those are two completely different things."

"You're right. And I know I'm overthinking everything because he makes me so incredibly happy." Hope walked with Bree towards the barn. "I really don't know what to do."

Bree set the horse brushes on a shelf. "For what it's worth, the guy is crazy about you. I've seen the way he watches you. I'm sure you'll figure something out."

Hope remembered how it felt to be Bree's age, when life was much simpler. "I hope so," she said.

Her mind whirred as she headed back to the house. She knew she fit together with Silas, but somehow, she had to figure out how to fit his daughter into the picture as well. Sierra deserved someone who would be there for her. Not someone who flitted in and out of her life.

Hope headed to the kitchen and pulled out sliced ham and a block of cheese. She was spreading mayonnaise on a piece of bread when she landed on the perfect plan. It was time to get Silas on board.

CHAPTER 18

The girls chattered in the back seat, telling Silas all about their farm tour. He had been unsure what to expect when Rose told him about Bree's class. Now he was sad that Sierra had missed the first couple of days. Bree was teaching the girls to love the ranch and understand the hard work that went into keeping animals.

He felt his lips twitching as he thought about how much he had enjoyed his tour of the ranch as well. Holding Hope felt as natural as breathing. She fit in his arms like she was made for them. And kissing her? That was an activity he planned to do again and again.

Silas pulled into the driveway in front of Rose's house, stopping the car so the girls could climb out. He stayed in his seat for a minute to gather his thoughts. Rose could always read his face, and he wasn't ready to share what had happened with Hope. Not yet. He still wasn't sure what to think about it himself.

By the time he walked up the steps, his face was composed. He headed into the house to check on his sister and ask about a playdate for Sierra. The girls came to their grandma's house almost every day, but Sierra wanted to play at her cousin's house, where they had all their toys. She wanted to see Lacy's doll house and Chrissy's dinosaurs.

Rose was hugging the girls when Silas's phone vibrated in his pocket. He pulled out the phone, tilting it slightly away from Rose when he saw a text from Hope.

"I'll be back in a sec," he said. He headed towards the car, opening Hope's message. The message was short, but it sent a wave of worry through him.

Can we talk?

Is everything okay? He pushed send, his mind swirling. They had just seen each other, and he was certain they had left on a good note. What could have changed?

Yes. I have an idea I want to run by you.

Silas closed his eyes and leaned against the hood, tilting his head back to study the sky. He wanted to drive back to the ranch immediately, but he was going to have to play it cool in front of Rose.

Give me ten.

Silas headed back into the house, feeling like a teenager that was trying to sneak out. He stuffed his phone back into his pocket and headed to the family room, where the girls were already putting dinosaurs on every flat surface in the room.

"Grrr." Sierra said. She ran to him, holding a bright

orange triceratops with green spikes running down the back.

"Oh no," Silas said, holding his hands out in front of him. "Don't eat me."

"Those ones don't eat people," Chrissy called. She was pulling out a bin filled with small tea cups.

"What is happening?" Silas asked, looking at Rose.

"Dinosaur tea party. We do them almost every day."

Silas watched while the girls arranged the dinosaurs in a circle around the coffee table. Lacy handed Sierra a handful of saucers.

"Make sure each dino gets one," she said. "The big dinos get two."

Sierra beamed while she carefully set a small saucer in front of each dinosaur. Chrissy followed behind with the tea cups.

"You do this every day?" Silas asked, bewildered when Lacy began to pour water into each cup.

"Yep." Rose looked over her shoulder at him. "Do you have any errands you want to run? Tea parties usually last for a while. I can watch the girls while I rest on the couch."

"Are you sure?" Silas didn't tell Rose that he was very eager to call Hope. He shrugged his shoulders. "I guess I have some things I can catch up on."

"I'm positive." Rose called to Sierra. "Sierra, honey. Do you want to play here while your dad does some work?"

"Yes!" Sierra called. Her cousins cheered.

"Come back in a couple of hours," Rose said. "I'll call if we need you sooner."

Silas knelt by Sierra's side, giving her a hug. "Make sure the dinosaurs play nice," he said. He kissed her forehead and hugged his nieces. "I'll see you in a little while."

The sun glinted off his windshield when he climbed back into the car. He dialed Hope's number and turned the car towards the Matthews Ranch, setting the phone in speaker mode while he drove.

"That was fast," she said. "Is now a good time to talk?"

"I just dropped Sierra off at Rose's house. I have a couple of hours."

"Oh perfect. I'd love to talk in person. Can you meet me at the ranch?"

Silas held back a laugh. "I'm already on my way."

* * *

THE FOLLOWING afternoon Silas helped Sierra to pull her hair up into ponytails. She handed Silas pink ribbons to tie on each side.

"I want to look pretty for your friend."

Silas tweaked her nose. "You look pretty every day, Pumpkin."

A smile beamed across Sierra's face until she looked in the mirror. "What if I forget her name, Daddy? Or if I spill something on my shirt?"

"Did you forget her name?"

Sierra shook her head. "Her name is Hope and she's Bree's big sister."

"Exactly." Silas pulled the ribbon straight before kissing

the top of Sierra's head. "You have already met her a couple of times. Didn't she help Bree show you the horses?"

Sierra grinned. "Her favorite one is the all black horse with a white nose."

"See? You already know something about her. Do you want to know something fun?"

"What?" Sierra wiggled in her chair before she jumped down.

Silas could feel her scrutiny. As much as he wanted everything to go perfectly, he couldn't help but worry. Getting Sierra's approval was vital for any relationship he started. If Sierra didn't like her, Silas would have to walk away.

The thought of leaving Hope sent a pang straight to his heart. He was falling back in love with her, but to Sierra, she was mostly a stranger. Somehow, he had to slow his feelings down.

"That one is my favorite, too." Silas checked his own hair in the mirror, purposely running a hand through it so it stuck up on the side. "How do I look?"

Sierra giggled and tugged at his shirt, pulling his head down to her level. "You look too silly." She patted the side of his head.

"Remember that Hope doesn't care what we look like. Even with silly hair. Hope isn't going to notice if you spill crumbs on your shirt or if the wind blows your hair away. All she wants is to have some fun together."

"At a picnic?" Sierra ran to the bedroom and came back with her stuffed kitty. "Can Simmy come, too?"

They didn't usually bring Sierra's stuffed animals with her. That was something she asked for when she was nervous. Silas studied his daughter's face. "I don't want anything to happen to Simmy while we're gone. Can he come in the car and wait for us while we play at the park?"

Sierra nodded her head. "Coco, too?"

"Yes. Coco, too." Silas checked his watch while Sierra ran to her room to get her stuffed monkey. If they would help her to feel more comfortable, he was happy to let them tag along. Hope would understand if they were a couple of minutes late.

The nerves didn't kick in until Silas pulled into the parking lot. He climbed out of the car and said a quick prayer, asking the Lord to help Sierra and Hope to make a connection. The loud laughter of children playing on the playground reminded him that Sierra was pretty easy going. Silas was treating their time together like a job interview instead of the playdate it was meant to be.

A quick scan of the parking lot told Silas that Hope wasn't there yet. He waited for Sierra to climb out of her car seat, smiling as she buckled Coco and Simmy into her spot. They would stand guard until Sierra came back to get them.

They headed towards the playground, Sierra running ahead to climb on the play structure. Ten minutes later, Silas was beginning to wonder if he and Sierra had been stood up. He scanned the parking lot, looking for Hope's car, but it wasn't there.

Silas followed Sierra to the swingset, pushing his

daughter higher and higher while she giggled uncontrollably. He was stepping out of the way of the swing when Hope called.

"Are you guys still at the park?" She sounded breathless, like she had just run to the phone.

"Yep. I'm pushing Sierra on the swing." He pushed down the twinge of annoyance. Hope wouldn't be calling if she was almost there.

"I'm sorry I'm not there, yet. Emily asked me to bring her something from the house. I showed up at the doorstep to drop off the bag and ended up helping to deliver a baby llama."

"You're kidding, right?"

"I'm serious." Hope paused. "How do you feel about a change of plans? Does Sierra want to meet a newborn llama?"

"Absolutely. We'll head on over."

Fifteen minutes later, Silas pulled to the front of Emily's llama therapy center. He had been confused when he first heard about the place. He didn't understand how working with an animal would help someone with their problems. Now he understood how spending time with the animals helped people to open up.

Hope was waiting for them, a huge smile on her face. He wanted to grab that beautiful face and cover it with kisses, but instead he settled for a quick hug.

He held Sierra's hand as Hope bent over to greet her. "Hi Sierra. I'm sorry about missing our picnic."

"It's okay." Her eyes flicked up to Silas and then back to Hope. "Do you have a baby llama?"

"We do." Hope straightened up, wiping her hands down her jeans. "She was just barely born, but Emily says it's okay to come see her if we're really quiet. We don't want to startle the mom."

Sierra nodded, her eyes deep with concern. "I can be quiet." She followed after Hope, clinging tightly to Silas's hand.

They walked across a small field, stopping several feet back from where Emily stood. Hope knelt down beside Sierra and pointed. "That's Emily. She takes care of these llamas. The momma is Wren and that is her baby." A small brown mound lay on the ground, surrounded by the herd.

"Why are there so many llamas by her?"

Even Silas was surprised. The other llamas in the herd were sniffing the baby, gently nuzzling her. He didn't think they would be so curious.

"They are all her aunts and uncles. They want to say hi."

"Doesn't it bother the mom?" Silas asked.

Hope shook her head. "Emily says it's what they do. I never thought I'd help deliver a baby in a crowd of llamas. That was a first for me."

Sierra tugged on the edge of Silas's shirt to get his attention. "Why isn't the baby moving?"

They both looked at Hope.

"I'm not a vet, but I think the baby is just resting. She has to get used to the world."

Emily looked over her shoulder and then headed back

towards them. She glanced at Sierra and then lowered her voice to speak to Hope. Silas leaned in so he could hear her better. "I thought the baby would be starting to walk now. Hazel is on her way to check her out."

Sierra looked up. "Why isn't she walking now? And what will Hazel do?"

Silas held back a groan. He knew Emily was trying to protect his daughter, but Sierra had excellent hearing. What was he supposed to tell his daughter? He was struggling to find the right words when Hope knelt down beside Sierra.

"Did your dad tell you that I grew up on a ranch?"

"Like the one Bree lives at?"

"Exactly. That's where I grew up when I was a little girl. I've seen a lot of baby animals born. Most of the time they are strong and healthy. Animals know what to do to help their babies. But sometimes, a baby isn't quite as strong as we want them to be."

"Like this baby?" Sierra's eyes were wide, but her voice was steady. She was handling the situation well.

"Exactly. Just like this baby. Hazel is a vet. She helps the animals who are having a hard time."

The way Hope knelt next to Sierra sent a surge of gratitude through Silas. She wasn't treating his daughter like a young girl who was in the way. Instead, she was speaking to her with respect. Sierra rested her hand on Hope's arm.

"Is the baby going to die?"

Silas hated how small her voice sounded. A seven-year-old girl shouldn't be worrying about if an animal was going to live or die. He knelt down by Sierra's other side, but Hope was already speaking again.

"Sometimes the babies die, and it is really sad. I think this little girl is just sleepy." Hope looked at Emily. "What if we try rubbing her down?"

Silas watched as Hope took charge. She grabbed a towel out of a canvas bag and walked to the llama's side. Together, she and Emily began to dry the baby's wool coat, gently working the towels in circles up and down her small body.

Sierra grabbed Silas's hand. "Are they hurting the baby?"

"No, Pumpkin. I think they're helping her to get warm."

Hope whispered to Emily and then glanced their way. "You guys are doing a great job of staying back so Wren doesn't get scared. There is one job you can help with, if you'd like."

A smile beamed across Sierra's face. "We get to help, Daddy."

Silas squeezed his daughter's shoulder. "What would you like us to do?"

Hope and Emily both grinned. "Miss Sierra. Would you like to name the baby?"

CHAPTER 19

Excitement spread across Sierra's face as she looked to her dad for permission. Hope watched them out of the corner of her eye while she rubbed the llama's wool. She was hoping all the baby needed was to get the blood pumping through her veins.

"I'm good at naming animals," Sierra said.

"I thought you might be." Hope rubbed down the llama's neck to her back. The baby still wasn't moving much. As Hope tried to warm the baby, she began to silently pray. *Lord, please help this baby girl to be okay. I don't want Sierra to watch her die.*

Hope was trying to make friends with Sierra. Not traumatize her. Five seconds after Hope said amen, the baby began to kick and squirm.

A wave of relief crashed through Hope's body, almost bringing her to her knees with gratitude. Instead, she headed for Silas. He was giving her a look that said he knew how dicy that had been.

"Nice save," he whispered.

"What did they save?" Sierra asked.

Hope knelt down by Sierra's side once more. "Remember how I said Mrs. Hazel can help the baby animals?"

Sierra nodded.

"Well, now she won't have to help the baby. Look."

Hope pointed to the baby, who was pushing up from the ground with her back legs. A few tries later, the llama was standing on wobbling legs. Hope felt another surge of relief.

They were watching the baby stumble around when Hope felt a small tug on her hand. She looked down to see Sierra with a small frown on her face.

"What's wrong, sweetheart?"

Hope studied the little girl's face as she scrunched her forehead to think. There were traces of Silas in his daughter, from the way her mouth turned up in the corners to the shape of their straight noses. Hope had been around the two of them together a few times now, but her focus had always been on Silas. It was time to get to know Sierra.

"She needs a name, but I don't know which one is good."

"Do you have any ideas yet?" Hope gave Sierra's hand a reassuring squeeze.

"I like Lilly or Leena." Her lips quivered. "But what if I pick the wrong one?"

"I don't think that's possible. They are both great names." Hope hugged Sierra's shoulders. "Do you see that llama?"

She pointed to a tan llama nuzzling the baby. "That one is named Cupid. Do you know what a cupid looks like in most books?"

Sierra covered her mouth to hide a giggle. "It's a big fat baby with diapers."

"Exactly. Does that llama look like a big fat baby to you?"

Sierra shook her head. "No."

"It's a silly name, but it fits him just fine. Names can be silly."

Her smile was warming Hope's heart. It had been a while since she had been around the sweet innocence of a younger child. She caught Silas watching his daughter. The expression on his face was clear to read. He adored his little girl.

"I don't know about you," Silas said, "but I'm starving. How about you pick a name and we get to our picnic?" He bent down and Sierra climbed onto his back.

"I like Leena," Sierra said. "Is that one okay?"

"That's a perfect name."

Emily joined them, dumping the towels on top of the sack. "Would you like to come visit her again tomorrow?"

The smile that beamed across Sierra's face said it all. Hope knew she had made the right decision in asking Silas to bring Sierra over.

"Thanks again for your help, sis." Emily gave Hope a

quick hug. "And thanks for helping Leena to get the best name ever." She gave Sierra a high five.

"You're welcome," Sierra said.

Hope walked next to Silas on their way to the car. He made it halfway across the field before he froze. "Oh no. I think I lost Sierra."

Sierra giggled from Silas's back.

"Uh oh," Hope said, playing along. "Do you think she went to live with the llamas?"

Silas held a hand over his eyes to look across the field. "I do see a lot of animals out there. Can you see her?"

Sierra began laughing out loud and tapping Silas's shoulder.

Hope bent over to study the ground. "I think I hear her giggle. Maybe she's playing with the flowers."

"I'm right here," Sierra said.

Silas winked at Hope. "Do you think I left her at the park?"

Sierra was rocking back and forth on her dad's back, now. Hope dropped back slightly and held a hand behind Sierra so she could catch her if she started to slip.

"I hope not. I really wanted to spend time with her today." They were almost to the car now.

Silas was starting to open the door when Hope stopped him. "Uh, Silas? I think something is on your back."

He spun in a circle, looking over his shoulder. "What is it? A bug?"

Silas hopped back and forth from side to side while Sierra held on tight. Hope's heart was ready to burst from the cuteness of the two of them together. She wanted to be part of this little girl's world more than anything, but doubt was already creeping in.

Tomorrow, while Silas was getting breakfast for Sierra, she'd be back on a plane. Flying home for a couple of days had been amazing for her heart, but she had a commitment to fulfill. She was going to have to take advantage of every minute they had together.

"Do you want me to help brush it off?" Hope asked. Silas said yes, but Hope waited until Sierra nodded her head. Then she reached out and lifted her off Silas's back, spinning her in a circle before she set her on the ground with a hug.

Silas straightened up and shook his shoulders before turning to face them. His face lit up when he saw Sierra.

"Hey there, Pumpkin. Where did you come from?"

Sierra giggled. "I was right here, Daddy."

"Are you sure? Hope and I looked everywhere for you."

Sierra reached for Hope's hand, a huge smile spreading across her face. "She helped find me."

"Well, then." Silas slid his attention to Hope, reaching for her other hand. He squeezed it gently, sending a flutter straight to Hope's stomach. "I guess we'd better take her with us. I don't want you to get lost again."

Sierra climbed into the car, moving her stuffed animals to the side so she could buckle up. Hope started to walk to her truck, but Silas pulled her in the other direction. He swung her around once they reached the back of the car and pressed his lips to hers. Hope's body ached to lean in closer and run her fingers through his hair, but that wasn't why she was there.

"What about Sierra?" she asked. She could hear the hitch in her own voice.

Silas kissed her cheek. "Sierra," he said. He kissed the other cheek. "Sierra is busy telling Simmy and Coco about the llamas. We have a minute." He trailed a string of kisses down Hope's neck and back up to her lips.

Hope couldn't stop herself. She leaned into the kiss, trailing her hands across Silas's broad shoulders until she was cupping his neck. In the distance, Hope could hear a loud whoop. She knew Emily was watching them, but she didn't care. She was going to enjoy this moment.

All too soon, Silas was pulling away. "Are you ready for the park?"

"I am." Hope headed to her truck and climbed in, her heart pounding. She followed behind Silas's car and let her imagination go. In a dream world, she'd be sitting in the car next to Silas, and together they'd be taking their daughter to play.

Hope wanted to create a family with someone, but she had to keep her eyes and heart open. Silas was an incredible man, but choosing him didn't mean she'd automatically be Sierra's mom. There was a lot more to being a parent than liking someone's dad. Sierra would have to choose her, too.

Her thoughts were somber when she climbed out of the truck. It was time to start looking at the future with open eyes instead of just her heart.

* * *

THE LAUGHTER of children surrounded Hope and Silas as they sat on a blanket near the playground. Remains of lunch lay scattered around them, from empty sandwich bags to a half-eaten bag of chips. The blanket was covered with cookie crumbs where Sierra had been sitting, but now she was off chasing another little girl around the play structure.

Hope leaned against Silas, appreciating the warmth of the hand that rested against her hip. She watched Sierra, her stomach jumping every time Sierra did anything remotely dangerous.

Sierra ran in front of a swing, narrowly missing getting kicked in the head, and Hope strained forward. Silas's low chuckle beside her made her settle back into his arms.

"She's okay," he whispered. He kissed the top of Hope's head, and Hope tried to calm her racing heart.

"How can you stand it?"

Silas ran a thumb along her side. "What do you mean?"

"I mean, how can you stand watching Sierra run like that, narrowly avoiding all sorts of danger? By my count, she's almost gotten hurt a dozen times. And she scraped her knee that one time."

Hope leaned into Silas's side, reaching for his free hand. She needed to find a way to relax.

Silas watched Sierra for a moment before answering. "Being a parent is way harder than I thought it would be. When she was younger, I worried about every little bump she got. I bawled the first time I needed to take her to the doctor for something other than a routine checkup."

"What happened?" Hope couldn't imagine Silas in tears over a simple cut.

"I was boiling water for noodles while she was playing with her toys in the family room. I ran upstairs to get my cell phone, and came back just in time to see her reaching for the pot. She grabbed the side before I could stop her, and burnt her fingers."

Hope felt Silas shudder. She wrapped her hand around his, holding tight. There was pain in this memory that she couldn't take away, no matter how much she ached to. "That sounds awful."

Silas blew out his breath. "All things considered, it was a miracle she wasn't hurt worse. She could have pulled the entire pot of water down on herself. I think I cried harder than she did when the doctor was examining her fingers."

"I'm so sorry." Parenting was difficult enough to do with a partner. Hope could only imagine how hard it must have been to deal with it alone. "How long did it take for her to heal?"

"That's the crazy part. After just a couple of days, the blisters on her fingers began to fade. She seemed to forget the pain of it, although she still talks about the day she burnt her fingers. I'm the one who couldn't let go."

His voice was raw with emotion. Hope felt awful for prying. Silas lifted Hope's hand to his lips, gently kissing the back of her hand.

"I don't worry so much about the little things now,

because I know that she's tough. You saw how quickly she ran back to play after we kissed her boo boo better. I want her to be a strong little girl who can make wise decisions. If I'm always trying to save her, would I really be doing her any favors?"

Hope thought about her own parents and how she had been raised. If her parents had lived in fear of her getting hurt, she never would have learned to rope cattle, ride a horse, or drive a tractor. Letting her experience life is what gave her the confidence to stand on a stage in front of thousands.

"You know you're a pretty incredible dad, right?" Hope twisted her body so she could look Silas in the eyes. "Sierra is blessed to have you in her life, and so am I."

"Thanks." Silas brushed a kiss against her lips. "We're lucky to have you, too."

Hope turned her attention back to the playground, her heart racing until she spotted Sierra at the top of the slide, a huge smile on her face. "What's the best part of being a dad?"

"That's a hard one. Most of the time I feel inadequate. I know Sierra isn't getting the same opportunities as most of her friends because she doesn't have a mom in her life. I think the best part is watching her face life each day with optimism. She's a bright light every day, no matter what she's dealing with."

Hope's mind was racing. She knew dating Silas would come with responsibilities, but she hadn't really thought things all the way through. What if she said or did something to make Sierra's life harder? That wouldn't be fair to Silas or Sierra.

A weight settled on Hope's shoulders, pushing some of her happiness to the side. Was she living in a fantasy world?

Silas seemed to sense the shift in her mood. "What's wrong? What did I say?"

"Nothing. I'm going to miss you when I go back on tour. That's all." It wasn't the entire truth, but it also wasn't a lie. Hope was going to miss him dreadfully.

The wind blew a strand of hair across Hope's face. She moved it to the side, grateful for the chance it gave her to swipe at the tear welling in the corner of her eye.

Silas pressed his chin to her shoulder, turning his head so he could kiss her cheek. "I wish you didn't have to go so soon."

Hope was turning to face him when a sharp cry from the playground made Silas go stiff. He was up and running before Hope could even process how he recognized the cry of his daughter from all the other children's happy shrieks.

Silas came back with Sierra in his arms. "It's her stomach again," he said.

He tried to put Sierra down on the blanket beside Hope, but Sierra shook her head, crying harder while clinging to her dad.

"No, Daddy. I don't want Hope. I want you."

Hope could read the frantic look in Silas's eyes when he pulled Sierra back to his chest. Hope rose to her feet and reached for his arm but his body was stiff.

"We've got to get to the doctor. Can you take care of all this?" He jerked his head towards the picnic.

"Of course. Get her help."

Hope watched in silence as Silas walked away, Sierra's small head bobbing as he carried her to the car. She waited for him to turn and wave, but he folded into his seat and drove away without so much as a backwards glance.

There was a sting that remained, a gentle reminder that as much as Silas loved spending time with Hope, his daughter would always come first. It was how Hope expected things to be, but she couldn't help but wonder if there was really room for her in their lives.

She packed up the picnic, her thoughts racing as she tried to figure out what to do next. If Silas was hurt, she'd be by his side. It was different with Sierra being in pain. Did Hope have any right to reach out?

The last of the crumbs were shaken off the blanket before Hope settled on a plan. Her nerves warned her to run away, but her heart wanted to give things one more try. She folded the blanket and set it in the truck before pulling out her phone. It was time to be brave.

CHAPTER 20

Instead of heading home, Silas drove straight to the doctor's office. He had never seen Sierra so pale. Something was really wrong, and he was going to stay in the office until they found a solution. He was done with vague answers that kept his daughter in pain.

A small part of his brain registered that he was leaving Hope behind to clean up their picnic, but he was sure she wouldn't mind. She understood how important Sierra's health was to him. He'd call later to update her on the situation and apologize.

Sierra was whimpering when he pulled her out of the car. That was unusual for his daughter, who usually hid how she was feeling. The fact that she was crying told him just how serious it was.

"We're almost there, Pumpkin." The knot in Silas's stomach was tight, a coil of strings knotting together into a clump that would be impossible to untangle.

Carrying Sierra through the doors, Silas's stomach dropped. This was the same doctor he had been working with since they had come home to visit. He didn't know how to help Sierra any better than the doctors in the city had.

Silas paused in the entryway, the double doors staying open while he stood on the stoop. He bowed his head and said an urgent prayer, begging the Lord to clear his thoughts so he would know what to do.

When the answer came to his mind a moment later, Silas didn't hesitate. He swung around and took Sierra back to the car, buckling her in.

"Why are we leaving, Daddy? That doctor helps me." Sierra's eyes were filled with large tears.

"He does," Silas said. He wasn't going to tell Sierra his frustrations about the doctor. "Do you know how sometimes we see the doctor and he makes you better for a little bit?"

Sierra nodded, wiping her eyes with the back of her hand.

"I'm taking you to a new doctor. Hopefully he will make it so you don't have tummy goblins ever again."

Silas gunned it through a yellow light, and swerved into the hospital parking lot five minutes later. He didn't know why the Lord had led him to the hospital, but he wasn't going to question it.

Every step towards the entrance lifted a piece of worry from Silas's heart. He wasn't sure what he'd find inside, or if there were any new answers waiting. All he knew was that he was in the right place for Sierra. The Lord was whispering peace to his mind.

A slender woman wearing a lime green shirt greeted them at the front desk. "You're in luck," she said, as she led them back to an examination room. "We have Dr. Kline making the rounds today. He's the best with young children."

Another weight lifted off Silas's shoulders as he listened to the receptionist prattle on. From what he could gather, Dr. Kline was the leading pediatric gastroenterologist on the west coast. He occasionally came to the hospital to give back to the community where he had trained.

Sierra was curled up on the chair with Simmy and Coco when the doctor entered the room. His face broke into a large smile and he reached into his front pocket, pulling out a small brown monkey.

"I was hoping someone would bring a friend for Joey to meet. Would you like to introduce your animals to him? He's kind of shy."

Sierra reached for the monkey, and soon she was prattling to her toys while Dr. Kline listened to Silas. Silas gave the doctor a brief rundown of the various tests they had done. He could hear the frustration pouring out as he spoke of one test after another yielding no results.

The doctor was silent after Silas stopped speaking. He typed a couple more things into the chart, and then lowered his glasses. "I know how frustrating it can be to not find answers. The problem is that sometimes we focus on one area, but the answer lies in a different part of the body."

Silas nodded. He had heard that all before.

Dr. Kline continued. "Are you open to me running a few tests that I don't see on her charts yet?"

Silas wanted to grab Sierra and run, but he tried to have faith. If the Lord had led him to the hospital, there was most likely a reason why. He gave his permission and settled in for a long afternoon.

* * *

SIERRA WAS COMING BACK from her final test when Silas got a text message from Hope.

How are things going?

He wasn't sure what to tell her. Sierra had been being incredibly brave, but Silas was running out of patience. Every test seemed to hurt more than help. He wanted nothing more than to have someone by his side, telling him that he was doing the right thing for his daughter. Instead, he was doubting every decision.

She's a trooper, and I'm a mess.

There was a deep fatigue weighing down on Silas's body. He looked up from his phone when Dr. Kline entered the room.

The doctor sat down on a stool, rolling it over to the computer. "I want to thank you for being patient with me. I know that was a lot of tests." He rested his hand on Sierra's shoulder. "You did such a good job. So did Simmy and Coco."

"And Joey." Sierra hadn't put the small monkey down since she had been handed him.

"Yes. And Joey. I'm proud of you guys." He turned to Silas. "I think I found the source of her pain."

Silas slumped back against his chair. He wanted to believe the doctor, but he had been told that before. "What do you think is wrong with her?"

* * *

Two hours later, Sierra was being wheeled back for a same day surgery. Silas watched her go, sending her every ounce of faith he could muster. He felt hollow, and the day was far from over.

He had filled his family in on what was happening. His mom offered to come sit with him, but Silas downplayed his worries.

"She'll be fine," he'd said. "It's just a routine procedure."

Now, he was questioning his wisdom in being alone. He watched Sierra's tracking number on the display board next to the reception desk, gritting his teeth when it moved from pre-op to op. She was heading into surgery, and there was nothing he could do.

He was pacing the room for the third time when a pair of arms wrapped around his waist, hugging him from behind. Almost instantaneously, he could breathe again.

"How did you know I'd need you?" he asked, turning to face Hope.

Hope stroked a line from his shoulder down to his wrist. "I haven't stopped worrying since you ran off with Sierra. I figured that if I was that worried, you must be going out of your mind."

Silas pulled her close, hugging her to his chest while he stroked her hair. "You have no idea." He closed his eyes, trying to feel some of Hope's peace. "It's the first time she's been somewhere that I can't go. I won't be there to help if something goes wrong in that room."

"I know." Hope rubbed a circle on his back, her breathing steady.

"What if someone makes a mistake, or she gets scared, and I'm not there to hold her hand?" His panic rolled beneath the surface, a monster threatening to pull him under. Then he remembered who he was talking to. Hope's dad had passed away when she was younger. The doctors hadn't been able to help him.

He studied Hope's face, looking for any signs of distress, but she was calm. She met his gaze, her eyes steady. "Silas, I don't have the right words to say. I have never been a mom, but I've seen a lot of people I love go through hard things. Sierra is a brave girl, and from what I've seen, she's a fighter."

Silas nodded. He let Hope pull him to a small couch near the edge of the room.

"You told me you felt like you should bring Sierra here, right?"

"Yeah." He plopped down on the smooth, leather seat.

"Well then, I have to believe that the Lord is in charge. If he wanted your daughter to be here, it stands to reason that he'll guide the hands of the doctors who are helping her."

She held a hand to his cheek and Silas leaned into her warmth. He wanted to believe her words, but he couldn't.

"Sometimes people die. What if it's her time to go?" The thought of a world without Sierra in it made his stomach churn. He looked at Hope, waiting for her to speak the words that would calm his heart.

She didn't meet his eye. Instead, she stared off towards the operating board, blinking furiously.

With a sinking heart, Silas realized how much it must cost Hope to be in the waiting room with him. He wasn't sure where her dad had been taken after his accident, but the town was small. It had probably been this very hospital.

Hope's voice was soft when she spoke. "If it's her time to go, it will hurt a lot. You'll feel like the air has been punched from your body, and you'll have to fight for every breath."

Silas felt selfish for wanting Hope to be there. She shouldn't be stuck in a hospital, waiting beside him while she remembered the worst memories of her life.

She took a deep breath. "I don't know what it's like to be a parent losing a child, but I do know what it's like to be a daughter losing her dad. Silas, if it really is her time to go, it's going to be awful. I wish I could say otherwise, but I can't. A piece of you will go missing, and you'll never be the same again."

Hope was talking about Silas's present, but he knew she was really talking about her past. He pulled her close, resting his cheek against her head. "I'm sorry, Hope. I didn't think about what this would do to you."

She pressed her hand to his knee. "I'm okay. For what it's worth, I don't think it is Sierra's time to go. I think it's her time to heal. I can see that girl taking on the world. I, for one, can't wait to see what she does with her life."

Silas blew out his breath, letting the worry from the day roll off his shoulders. He kissed the top of Hope's head. "You're pretty incredible. You know that, right?"

"Thanks. So are you." Hope smiled at him, and Silas felt another piece of worry melt away. He had been raising Sierra by himself for so many years, he wasn't sure how to let anyone else help. Hope was making the burden easier to share.

Another hour later, the nerves were kicking up again. Sierra should have been in recovery by now, but the screen showed her still in the operating room. Something was wrong. Even Hope was starting to fidget beside him.

"What time did you say she'd be done?" she asked.

"She was supposed to be done a half hour ago. I thought I'd hear from the doctor by now."

Hope dragged him to the receptionist desk. "Can we get an update on patient 2970, please?"

The man at the desk didn't look up. "Patient's info is on the board. You can watch the progress there."

Silas resisted an urge to shake the guy. "I've been watching the board. Her surgery is taking way longer than they told me it would. Is there any way to check that everything is okay?"

There must have been something in Silas's voice because the guy looked up, a frown on his face. "What is your relationship to the patient?"

"I'm her dad." Silas clenched Hope's hand.

"Let me check." It took just a second for the guy to dial the number of some mysterious person in the back. He gave Sierra's patient number and then waited. A moment later, his face fell. He hung up the phone, schooled the expression on his face, and looked up, but it was too late. Silas was spiraling downwards into a pit of despair.

People didn't get that look on their faces unless something was seriously wrong. Silas was dimly aware of the man talking to him, but he was falling into a dark tunnel. He could barely register Hope pulling him back to a chair and pressing against his shoulders until he sat down.

"Put your head between your knees," she was saying, but his mind couldn't focus.

Hope left his side. When she came back, he was aware of a cold washcloth being pressed against the back of his neck and the insides of his wrists.

He gasped, and looked up, the fog momentarily abating. "What are you doing to me?"

"Sorry," Hope said. "It's a trick my roommate from college taught me. Something about how cold helps calm the nerves. I don't actually know what it does, but I know it worked for me whenever I lost my mind."

This brought a smile to Silas's face, which quickly faded. "Did you see that guy's expression? He looked like he was about to tell me my puppy got hit by a car."

Hope grabbed both of his hands, pulling his attention to her. "You didn't hear what he said. It isn't a problem with Sierra. It's a problem with them not updating the patient boards."

"Seriously?" Silas wanted to march over to the desk and give the guy a lecture about proper facial expressions.

"Yeah. He says she's in recovery, and they'll be out to get you any minute."

Silas barely had time to process the words before a nurse was heading towards him.

"Mr. Foster?"

Silas nodded. He reached for Hope's hand, his nerves on edge. He wanted to trust that everything was okay with Sierra, but he wouldn't be calm until he could see her face.

"I'm here to take you and your wife back to see your daughter. She's just waking up from the anesthesia so she may be a little groggy. I think she'll be happy to see you both."

Hope froze beside Silas.

He gave her hand a reassuring squeeze before looking at the nurse. "She's not my wife."

The nurse glanced at their hands. "My mistake. Anyway, Sierra is ready to see you."

Silas pulled Hope up and began to follow the nurse. She planted her feet, shaking her head.

"Sierra needs to see her daddy. Not his random girlfriend."

Hope was so much more than that to him, but there wasn't time to argue. Silas needed to be by Sierra's side.

He wrapped his arms around Hope and pressed his forehead to hers. "I couldn't have done it without you. Thanks for being here."

"I'm glad I could be. Now, go see your baby girl. We can talk later."

Silas didn't need any more encouragement. He followed the nurse through a set of doors, waiting to see if his instincts in bringing her to the hospital had been right. Only time would tell if Sierra was really healed. He prayed she was, because he never wanted to go through another day like this again.

CHAPTER 21

Hope kept a smile plastered on her face when she walked out of the hospital, even though she was ready to cry. She never knew who would be watching. Sure enough, she was almost to her car when a woman stopped her.

"You're Hope Matthews, right? My girls and I are huge fans. Can I get an autograph?"

Signing autographs was something Hope didn't think she'd ever get used to. It was crazy to think that people actually cared enough about her music to even notice who she was.

"Of course," she said. She pulled a pen out of her purse and took the paper that the woman held out. "Who would you like me to make it out to?"

"Ashley and Meg, please."

Ashley and Meg,

Never stop reaching for your dreams!

Hope

She added a swirl to the end of her name and handed the paper back with a smile.

"Thank you so much," the woman said. "They are going to be so sad they missed you."

"You can tell them I said hi. Take care." Hope walked away from the woman, grateful that she hadn't asked why Hope was leaving the hospital. In a world filled with gossip, she was learning to appreciate anyone who respected her privacy.

Rain began to patter down, causing Hope to run the rest of the way into the parking garage. She climbed into her truck and jammed the locks down before bending to rest her head on the steering wheel. There were too many emotions clamoring for attention, and Hope wasn't sure which one to focus on first.

As much as she was embarrassed to admit it, she was jealous. Silas had been glad to see her, but the second the nurse arrived, Hope could feel his energy shifting. He was there for Sierra, and Hope was nothing more than an afterthought.

A rational person would understand that Silas would always choose his daughter first. He was her dad, and it was his job to protect her. The problem was that Hope couldn't figure out where she'd fit into his and Sierra's lives.

In her most honest moments, she had to admit that when dreaming about her ideal man, dating a single dad wasn't top of the list. Relationships were complicated enough when just two people were involved.

The matter was more complicated because she knew a version of Silas that had existed before Sierra was part of the picture. In high school, Silas would drop everything he was doing to comfort Hope. Now that attention was focused on a seven-year-old girl.

Part of the reason Hope was falling for Silas was because she could see all those tender sides of him. Love radiated every part of his voice when he talked about Sierra. Watching them together in person was even sweeter.

Hope had begun to dream about a future with Silas, but she wasn't sure where her place would be. She wouldn't be starting a life with a man she could get to know over the years before deciding to have children. She'd be starting a life as an instant family.

The rain pounded against Hope's truck when she pulled out of the parking garage onto the street. Rivulets of rain cascaded down the windshield, overpowering the wipers that swished back and forth in ineffective arcs. She was halfway home when a text came through. It was a good excuse to pull to the side of the road.

The text was a selfie of Silas with his head bent close to Sierra's. Sierra's eyes were droopy, but she was smiling as she gave a thumbs up to the camera.

The doctor says everything went well.

A wave of relief washed over Hope. She had assumed

Sierra would be fine, but a small part of her had been worried that Silas was going to get bad news.

I'm so glad. How long until you can take her home?

Hope held her phone out, waiting for Silas's answer to come through. Three dots flickered on the screen, but his reply never appeared.

Not wanting to be stuck out in the rain any longer than she had to, Hope headed for home. She spent the rest of the drive talking to the Lord.

Lord, you know how I feel about Silas. When it's just the two of us, I see a future together. But it isn't just the two of us. Sierra would be part of this picture too. Honestly, I'm scared to death to even pretend like I know how to raise a little girl.

Please guide my mind and my emotions. I'd rather break my own heart than be the cause of more pain in their lives. You know what's best for all of us. I'm putting my faith in your hands. Amen.

As she came up the road to the house, the rain stopped and there was a break in the clouds. Brilliant sunlight framed the opening, casting rays of light down to the earth. Hope took it as a sign from the Lord that He was listening. She didn't know what the answer would be, but she felt the peace of knowing he was in charge.

Bree was waiting to pounce when she walked in the door. "Where have you been? Emily said you helped deliver the baby. Is she adorable?"

She was bouncing on her toes again, and Hope was pretty sure she knew what question was coming next.

"So, do you want to go visit Baby Leena with me? I'm going anyway, but it would be more fun if you came along."

She finally stopped to take a breath, and Hope wrapped an arm around her sister's shoulders. "Yes, I'll go with you. Emily said it's okay?"

Bree nodded. "She invited me herself."

Hope pulled out her phone to double check that she hadn't missed a text from Silas, but the dots were still there. He hadn't answered her yet.

"Let's go."

* * *

THE SUN ARCHED towards the horizon but Hope couldn't tear Bree away from the llamas. Hope leaned against a fence post to watch as Bree snapped more photos.

She looked up when Emily came to stand beside her. "Things looked pretty chummy today between you and Silas. How's that relationship going?"

Hope wasn't used to having an older sister to confide in. She turned to face Emily. "Are you asking to be polite, or do you really want to know? Because I could use some advice." She had debated about talking to Emily when they arrived, but the timing hadn't felt right.

Emily called out to Bree. "I need Hope's help inside for a minute. Are you okay keeping an eye on Leena?"

Bree's face lit up with a smile. "Yes. She's perfect."

"That should buy us a few minutes." Emily headed towards the center. "Come on in."

Hope followed Emily into a small office. A large canvas print from Porter and Emily's wedding day hung on one wall. Emily was looking straight into the camera, her eyes bright with excitement while she held a bouquet of flowers to her face. Porter was staring at Emily, and even through the photo, it was clear just how deeply he adored his wife. Love radiated from the picture.

That was the goal. Hope wanted to marry someone who looked at her the way Porter looked at Emily.

"What's going on?" Emily asked. "I thought you guys were in a great place when I saw you."

Hope rubbed her hand across the smooth desktop to calm her nerves. "If it was just the two of us, everything would be easy."

Understanding crossed Emily's face. "But he has a daughter."

"Exactly. The more I get to know Silas, the deeper I fall in love. And the deeper I fall in love, the more I realize that if we are going to have a future together, she's going to be part of it. Who am I to assume I have any right being part of Sierra's life? I leave for tour again in the morning. That isn't the behavior of a stable person." Emotion swelled in her voice.

"It's not like you're off on some wild bachelorette trip. What does Silas say?" Emily slid a box of tissues across the desk.

Hope pulled a tissue out, dabbing at her eyes. She didn't know why she was crying. It wasn't like Silas had asked her to choose between their relationship or the tour. He had been nothing but supportive.

"We haven't talked about it much. He knows how important my music is to me. We were going to spend the day together so I could get to know Sierra better, but she ended up in the hospital."

Emily jolted forward. "Is she okay? Do we need to do anything for them?"

Hope shook her head. "I don't think we can. She had another bad stomach ache when we were at the park, so Silas took her to the hospital. They ended up performing a minor surgery that is supposed to make the stomach aches stop."

"How is Silas doing?"

Hope pulled out her phone to check for a response, knowing there wouldn't be one. She would have felt the phone vibrate if he had replied. "He seemed fine when I left the hospital."

Emily could sense the hesitation in her tone. "Why do you sound like that's a bad thing? Don't you want things to be okay?"

Hope took a deep breath. "He said he was glad I was there, but as soon as they were finished with the surgery, he couldn't wait to get back to Sierra."

"That sounds like a normal reaction to me." Emily steepled her fingers together and rested her hands on the table. "I'm not little Leena's mom, but I've been watching her like a hawk all day to make sure she's okay. If I'm reacting that way to a baby animal, it makes sense that as a parent he'd be worried."

"I know. He's a really good dad."

"So what's the problem?"

Hope rubbed her jeans. "I recognize that I'm being petty, but I wanted to be there with him. I wanted to be standing by his side as Sierra woke up, but I knew I shouldn't be. I'm not her mom. I'm barely her friend. I can love Silas all I want, but I will always be competing for his attention. I volunteered to leave instead of making things awkward."

Emily was quiet for a minute. "I never met your dad, but Porter has told me a lot about him. From what he said, your dad practically worshiped the ground your mom walked on. Do you agree?"

"Yeah. He adored her."

"Did you feel any less loved when you were a child?"

"No." Hope could see where Emily was going.

"The thing I've learned about love is that I don't think it ever runs out. There always seems to be plenty to go around."

Hope took a deep breath. "I know that, in theory, but I don't know how to handle it in real life. We're barely dating, and I'm already stressing over being a bonus mom to this sweet little girl. I don't know if I can handle it. What if I say or do something wrong?"

Emily reached for her hand. "Hope, what if you are exactly the woman Sierra needs in her life? You could teach her to follow her dreams and not give up. You could show her an example of warmth and kindness. You could teach her that even though hard things happen, there is always good to be found in the world. You could help her to develop her faith in the Lord."

Hope dabbed at her eyes. Talking to Emily was exactly what she needed. "You know, you're going to be a pretty incredible mom when you and Porter are ready to start a family. You have so much wisdom to impart."

"Thanks." Emily slid a hand to her stomach. "You know, you aren't going to have to wait too long before you're an aunt."

"Really?" Hope's eyes lit up as she understood what Emily was implying. "Are you pregnant?"

Emily held a finger to her lips. "We're planning on telling everyone on Sunday. Can you keep the secret until then?"

Hope nodded her head, too overcome with emotion to speak. She grabbed Emily's hands. "I am so happy for you," she said. She brushed away a couple of tears.

"Thanks." Emily opened the desk drawer and pulled out two tiny pairs of crocheted cowboy boots. "We're going to slip these under Mom's dinner plate and see how long it takes for everyone to notice them."

"They are adorable!" Hope reached for the pink boots, gently running her hand over the edge. As she did, memories of the last time she thought she was going to be an aunt slammed into her mind. This wasn't the first time Porter was preparing to be a dad, but that time had ended in tragedy. "How is Porter handling things?"

Emily's smile dropped and concern filled her eyes. "He's excited, but I know he's worried. The last time he thought he was going to be a dad, his entire world fell apart. I think logically he knows I should be fine, but I don't think he'll breathe easy until the baby is in his arms."

Her eyes brightened. "I, on the other hand, am probably going to be the most spoiled pregnant woman ever. Porter is already going out of his way to make sure I have everything I could possibly need, including late night runs to the grocery store for ice cream."

The front door to the center banged open, and Bree's voice echoed down the hall. Hope tossed the boots back to Emily, who discretely shoved them into a drawer right before Bree came into the room.

"I'm handing babysitting duty back to you. Some of my friends want to hang out."

"I guess that's my cue." Hope pushed away from the desk and went to Emily's side, pulling her into a hug. "Thanks for the advice."

It wasn't until she was walking out with Bree that she realized she wasn't going to be home for the birth announcement. Emily had given her a gift by telling her the news first.

Hope's heart was lighter as she drove home, listening to her sister talk. Her personal life was complicated, but her family was doing well. At least she didn't have to worry about them when she got back on the road in the morning.

She didn't hear from Silas until she was brushing her teeth to get ready for bed. The text that came through included a long apology. The doctor had come in right when he was done typing, and instead of pressing send, he had exited out of messages. He couldn't figure out why Hope was ignoring him.

Hope changed into an old t-shirt and soft pajama bottoms and propped a pillow against her headboard to lean back on. She called Silas, her heart skipping a beat when his face filled the screen. He panned the camera over to show Sierra, sound asleep in her bed.

"Have you been sitting by her all night?" Hope whispered.

Silas nodded, and the video jumped around as he got to his feet and headed to his own room.

"I'm afraid to let her sleep. Her oxygen levels got low in the hospital so I'm keeping an eye on her. So far she seems to be breathing fine."

Hope wanted to brush the hair off his brow. "I'm glad she's okay, Silas."

"Me too. Are you ready to head out in the morning?"

It was hard to believe she had only been home for a couple of days. "I'm excited to keep touring. I'm going to miss you, though."

Silas leaned his head towards the phone. "You have no idea how much I'm going to miss you, too."

Hope stayed awake long after Silas hung up. Her thoughts scattered in a million directions but she was sure of one thing. No matter how complicated their relationship was, she was ready to fight for it.

She didn't know if she belonged in Silas or Sierra's life

long term, but she knew she wanted to try. She had given her heart to Silas once before, and he had shattered it. Now she had to trust that she could give it to him and he'd take care of it. They would work out the rest of the details as they went.

CHAPTER 22

Silas sat on a park bench, watching Sierra run with her new friend. It had been two weeks since Sierra's surgery, and from what Silas could see, the doctor had been right. The simple repair had made Sierra so much better. She hadn't had a single stomach ache since that day at the park with Hope.

Thinking about Hope sent an intense wave of longing that crashed over his body. He was back to late night phone calls and an occasional postcard from her. Each time Silas hung up the phone, he wanted to run to the airport and fly to wherever she was.

Sierra screamed, the sound of it sending a jolt of fear straight to Silas's heart until he realized that she was playing tag. The scream turned to giggles when her friend caught her.

He loved watching his daughter play. Spending the summer at home had given him a new perspective on being a parent. It had been nice to have help instead of doing everything alone.

Almost unbidden, his thoughts turned to Hope. He would give almost anything to have her sitting on the bench beside him. Being able to video call every day was a blessing, but it wasn't the same as sitting in the same room with her. He wanted to hold her hand while she told him about her day instead of sitting on the other side of a screen.

Their conversations had changed since Hope went back on tour. She seemed to be pulling away from him, and Silas couldn't figure out why. Whenever he asked, she said things were fine and tried to change the subject.

Thankfully, the tour was heading to Denver soon. Silas couldn't wait to surprise Hope. Maybe then, with her wrapped in his arms, he'd be able to figure out what was bothering her.

FIVE DAYS later Silas was checking into a hotel room near the concert venue. He wasn't sure where Hope would be staying, but he figured it would be somewhere near the arena. The desire to call her had him picking up his phone a dozen times, only to set it down each time.

His visit was a surprise, and Silas didn't want to ruin that. He wanted to watch Hope perform in her element, cheering along with the rest of her fans. Besides, she would be getting ready for the show, and probably didn't need any distractions.

An hour before the show began, Silas lined up at the venue. He held his barcode up to be scanned, and filed into the arena with hundreds of other people. There were large posters hanging from the ceiling above various vendor stands. Most of the pictures were of Ginny Brooks, but there were also a few vendor tables dedicated purely to Hope.

Silas's heart kicked up a beat while he made his way through the crowd to one of the tables. The vendor had T-shirts with Hope's face plastered across the front of them. She was holding a microphone and wearing a white cowboy hat. The fringed leather vest in the picture was something Silas was used to seeing on the days she called him from the limo.

He plunked his credit card down on the table, buying a large shirt for himself and an extra small one for Sierra. He also threw in a couple of refrigerator magnets. The guy taking his money grinned.

"Are you a big fan?" he asked.

Silas smirked. "The biggest." He wasn't about to tell the vendor that he knew Hope. That would be his secret for the night.

"Enjoy the show!" The man turned his attention to the next customer, and Silas pulled out his phone, snapping a picture of the large poster. He texted it to Rose and Mia.

Forty-five minutes until concert time.

Mia texted back immediately. **Don't embarrass yourself.**

His sisters had been teasing him non-stop about how he'd react when he saw Hope.

Are you guys sure I can't push past all the security guards and join her on the stage?

Rose sent a chain of laughing emojis. **That sounds like a great way to get kicked out of the concert.**

Good point. I'd hate to miss her singing. Silas gripped the bag tightly as he made his way into the arena.

Nervous energy followed him as he navigated down the stairs, getting closer and closer to the stage. He had been to concerts before, but somehow the entire arena felt gigantic when he imagined one woman filling the space. Admiration filled his thoughts. He had no idea where Hope found the confidence to sing for that many people.

People continued to pour through the doors, slowly filling the arena until it was packed with an excited crowd. Ten minutes before the concert was ready to begin, Silas felt his phone vibrate. He wasn't thinking about his actions when he pulled it out.

A photo of Hope filled the screen. She was standing in the dressing room, her hair and makeup done. **I have a feeling tonight's crowd is going to be epic.**

Silas started to type a response, but the girl next to him grabbed his arm.

"Is that Hope?" she asked.

"Uh." He wasn't sure what to say. There wasn't really

much point in denying that he knew her. "Yeah. She's a friend."

"No way." The girl smacked her friend to get her attention. "He knows Hope. Like in real life, knows her."

They both began to squeal, earning confused looks from the people around them. Silas could only imagine what their reactions would be if they knew he was dating her. They'd probably lose their minds.

A guy in the row behind Silas tapped his shoulder. "I didn't mean to eavesdrop, but do you really know her?"

Silas nodded. "We've been friends since high school."

"That is so cool." He leaned over to whisper to his date, who quickly turned her attention to Silas.

"If you know her, why aren't you backstage?" She raised an eyebrow like she didn't really believe him.

"I'm here to surprise her. I'll visit her after the concert."

Suddenly, his mouth went dry. In the matter of a few hours, he'd be holding Hope in his arms. He'd seen her on video calls after the concerts, but now he was going to get to feel that energy in person. It sent a thrill through his body.

The lights in the stadium dimmed, and an announcer's voice came through the speakers. Silas hurried to finish his message.

You deserve it. Be amazing.

He sent the text and then tried to pay attention to the announcer, but it was no use. There wasn't anything the man could say that was more important than Hope walking onto that stage.

There was a hush in the crowd that lasted for a heartbeat and then the chanting began. "Hope, Hope, Hope."

Silas broke into a grin as he joined in. If he was Hope's biggest fan, he'd better know how to greet her properly.

The lights blacked out, except for a small light in the center of the arena. Then the archway at the edge of the platform lit up with blue sparks and Hope ran onto the stage.

She waved to the crowd, taking Silas's breath away. This was a side of Hope he hadn't really seen before. She radiated a confidence that told the crowd she was happy to be there.

"Hello, Denver," Hope called, holding a microphone up to her mouth.

The cheering crowd was deafening.

"It's really good to see each of you." Hope scanned the crowd, and Silas could see why she was a favorite. She was making genuine eye contact with people in the crowd instead of looking over the tops of their heads. "This first song is for my dad."

She waited until the crowd grew silent, breathless with anticipation. They were eating right out of her hands. She strummed her hands down the guitar, the first few notes ringing through the air, and Silas closed his eyes, letting the music take him away.

To someone who didn't know Hope's background, the song was a cute song about a little girl who loved her dad. To someone who knew Hope well, it was easy to feel the longing woven through the versus. Especially when she sang of letting go of his hand.

Silas dabbed at the tears running down his cheek. She was mesmerizing.

The final notes died off, and the arena exploded with cheers. Hope's smile was genuine as she stood back, waiting for the applause to die down. She held the microphone up again, and before Silas had time to react, he was being taken on another journey through Hope's lyrics. Each song wove a different story.

All too soon, she held up her hand. "This is the last song for the night."

Silas groaned. He wasn't ready for her to be done.

She poured every part of her heart into the final song, and as she neared the end, she looked his way. Her eyes locked on his, the expression on her face impossible to read. He held his hand up to wave, and Hope blinked slowly before looking away.

His heart began to race. Was she angry with him for coming? She finished the song, and glanced his way again.

"You've been an incredible crowd tonight. How about we bring out the woman you're all waiting to see?"

The crowd began to chant Ginny's name, and Ginny ran onto the stage, giving Hope a high five on the way in.

Seconds later, Silas's phone buzzed with a text.

Am I losing my mind, or are you actually here?

He bit back a smile. **I'm here. You were incredible.**

The next text came through with instructions. **You have approximately two minutes to get to me so I can**

kiss your face properly. Make your way to the back entrance. Brody from security will show you to my dressing room.

Silas didn't hesitate. He apologized as he pushed past the people in his row, making his way to the stairs. When he reached the top, he began to run. In less than a minute, she was going to be in his arms.

* * *

SILAS SAT on a red couch in Hope's hotel suite. After covering his face with kisses, she had dragged him to the limo. After another round of kisses, she excused herself to get changed. She came out of the bathroom, and Silas had to pinch his arm to make sure she was real.

This was his favorite version of Hope. She had taken a quick shower, and now her hair hung in damp waves against the soft t-shirt she wore. Any traces of makeup had been washed away by the water. She looked like the woman he knew from home, and not the superstar that the crowd outside knew.

There was no hesitation as Hope folded onto the couch beside him, curling up by his side. Silas leaned in to inhale the intoxicating concoction of citrus and mint that came from her shampoo.

"Man, I've missed this," he said.

Hope wrinkled her nose. "You've missed me dripping my hair all over your shoulder?"

"Yes." He kissed the top of her head. "I'll happily let you get my shoulder wet if it means you are in my arms."

She grinned, lifting her lips to his.

The conversation was cut off for a minute while Silas obliged, kissing her softly. He broke off with a smile. "I know I just saw you singing a couple of hours ago, but it all feels so surreal. I can't believe you do that every weekend."

Hope stifled a yawn. "It's exhilarating every single time."

"Yeah. On an unrelated note, any chance you can snag one of your giant banners for me when the tour is over?"

Silas laughed when Hope flung an arm across her face. "Those are so embarrassing."

"Oh really? Why?" He couldn't see anything wrong with them.

"It's too weird seeing my face blown up that big. I don't think I'll ever get used to that."

Silas stroked a hand through her hair, gently wrapping a strand around his finger. "I don't know how you're used to any of this. How many dates are left?"

Silas knew exactly how long the tour was supposed to last, but he wanted to hear it from her lips.

"Three more weeks, and then I'm done." Her shoulders slumped. "I'm going to miss it."

"That makes sense." Silas shifted his arm so he could trail his finger down her cheek. "What are your plans afterwards?"

He tried to act nonchalant when he asked the question, but

his heart flew into overdrive. He and Hope hadn't really talked about how the future would look once she was done. Was she planning to move back to the city? Up until a few weeks ago, that's where Silas thought he'd be. Now he planned to stay in the country so Sierra could be with her cousins.

Hope turned her body so she could see his face. She rested her hands on his knees, her eyebrows creased with worry. "That all depends."

Silas held a hand over his chest, willing his heart to slow to a more steady beat. He was inches away from Hope's face. It would be so easy to kiss her instead of hearing an answer that could potentially break his heart.

"On what?" His mouth was dry.

The air in the room stilled as Hope raised her hand and rested it on his cheek. "It depends on you."

Silas sucked in his breath. The next words he uttered could change the course of his future. Was he ready to say them?

CHAPTER 23

Hope held her hand to Silas's cheek, his scruff rough against her finger tips. So much of the evening had felt like a dream, from seeing Silas in the audience to sitting in her room with him now. She held her breath, waiting for the words that would tell her he wanted her as part of his life.

Silas dropped his eyes, and Hope's heart sank when he blew out his breath. Her hand dropped to her lap. She looked at the space over his shoulder, unwilling to meet his eyes.

"My life is complicated. You know that I have Sierra, and that I'd do anything for her."

His words were soft, but Hope could hear the hesitation building in his voice. She had been worried about Sierra not liking her, and now she could see Silas getting ready to break her heart.

"I know. She's an amazing girl." Hope tried to keep her voice steady but she still couldn't meet his eyes.

"For years, I've had to balance my time between what's best for me, and what's best for her. Most of the time, I put all her needs before my own. It's what any good parent would do for a young child."

The moments with Silas were slipping away. He was going to say the words that ended it all, and Hope wasn't ready. She nodded her head, unable to speak.

Silas reached up to tuck her hair behind her ears. His touch was so gentle, it sent Hope's heart skittering through her chest. She leaned into his touch, memorizing the feel of his fingers as they brushed against her ear. It wasn't fair for him to be so gentle when he was getting ready to say goodbye.

"I learned something about myself when she was in the hospital."

Silas slid his hand to Hope's chin, lifting it gently until she had no choice but to look into his eyes.

"And what was that?" She didn't want to hear the answer. Not if it was the words that would take him away from her. She had worried that she was too unstable for Sierra to be around.

A smile lifted his lips. "I learned that sometimes, it's okay to put my needs first."

Yearning pierced her chest as his fingers trailed down her neck to brush against her collar bone. He slid his hand to her back.

"I don't know what your future looks like, but I

sincerely hope that it includes Sierra and me. I know I can live without you. I've raised Sierra on my own for years. It's something I'm good at doing."

His hand was moving back to her neck now, his fingers tangling in her damp hair while he pulled her close.

"I can live without you, but I don't want to. Not any more. I have a good life, but it is infinitely better with you in it. I know I'm asking you to come into my complicated world, but—".

Hope didn't let him finish the sentence. She wrapped her arms around his neck, closing the distance between their lips with a kiss.

"Complicated doesn't scare me," Hope said, pulling back. "If it involves you and Sierra, that is where I want to be."

The joy that lit Silas's eyes took Hope's breath away.

"In case you haven't figured it out, I'm insanely in love with you, Hope. We took a rocky path to get to this point, but I never stopped loving you. And if you let me, I'll spend the rest of my life showing you just how important you are to me."

Hope's eyes filled with tears. "I'll happily spend each day of forever by your side. I love you, too."

By the time Silas was done kissing her, Hope felt like she was floating on the ceiling. They had a lot to work out, but together, she knew they'd be able to handle whatever came their way.

* * *

THE FINAL DAY of the tour arrived, sending a swirl of emotions through Hope's body. She had just finished adjusting her vest when a knock sounded at the door.

Brody was standing outside, his hands crossed across his chest. "There are some people here to see you, Miss Matthews."

Hope took a deep breath. Fans usually didn't come backstage until after the concert, but she guessed they were switching things around because it was the last night of the tour. She stepped back to glance at her reflection, making sure she was ready for photos.

"You can let them in." Hope turned to greet her fans, and her jaw dropped. Instead of a bunch of eager people with cameras in their hands, there were only two people. They both wore t-shirts with her face plastered across the front of them, but they were missing the VIP badges that the fans usually wore.

Sierra ran to hug Hope's legs. "You look pretty," she said.

"So do you. I love your shirt." Hope winked at Sierra.

Silas stepped up to her side. "My turn." He reached for Hope's hand, spinning her in a slow circle before he lifted the hand to his lips. "I'd kiss you for real, but I don't want to mess up your makeup."

Joy flooded Hope's body. "You guys are here. I thought you said you couldn't come."

"I thought we couldn't either, but I got things worked out. We didn't want to miss your final night."

Hope wrapped her arms around her two favorite

people in the world, blinking back the emotion. Having them at the concert meant more to her than she thought it would.

Another knock sounded at the door, and Hope opened it to see Brody standing in front of it. "Sorry to interrupt again, but there's one more person here to see you."

A quick glance at the clock told her she had just a few more minutes until she was supposed to be heading for the stage. She held back a sigh of frustration. Another distraction meant less time with Silas and Sierra.

"Send him in."

A man in ripped jeans and a Ginny Brooks t-shirt entered the room.

"I'm Zeke Glenn," he said, holding out a hand.

The name was familiar, but Hope couldn't place him. "Nice to meet you. What can I help you with?"

Zeke held out a business card. "I own the recording studio which handles Ginny's music. I'd love to talk to you about getting some of your songs recorded."

Hope reached for the card, her mind spinning. "I'd like that a lot." She flipped the card over in her hand, reading his name in large letters.

"I don't want to keep you. I just wanted to make sure you know who I am when I call in a few weeks."

"It was nice to meet you. Talk to you soon." Hope's insides were dancing.

Zeke shook her hand and headed out the door, letting it shut with a soft click behind him.

She waited for just a second before she began to jump

up and down. She spun to hug Silas. "Do you know what this means?"

"I think it means you're going to be busy this year." Silas brushed a gentle kiss against her cheek. "I knew you could do it."

The future was coming together, with every piece falling into place. She had her career. She had the guy. And most importantly, she had the chance to be part of a family that she could love with all her heart.

Brody escorted Silas and Sierra out of the room. Hope knew he'd put them in the front row seats that were saved for their most important guests. Her heart was beating out of her chest. How did she get so lucky?

Hope leaned against the vanity, taking a minute to soak in everything that had happened over the past few months. Once she walked out the door, her final concert would begin.

CHILLY AIR BLEW through open windows as Hope walked through her apartment, closing the cupboards for the final time. She had spent the last week packing boxes, which Monroe had patiently carried to the moving truck that morning.

"I can't believe you're really moving home," he said. He leaned against the counter, wiping his brow.

"You know it's just a short drive away, right?" Hope

bumped her best friend's shoulder. "You and Felicity can come visit whenever you want."

"It won't be the same though."

Hope's smile faltered. "I know." She rested a hand on his arm. "I wouldn't have made it through all these years without you."

Monroe covered her hand with his own. "Yes, you would have. You are an unstoppable force, Hope Matthews. Nothing can hold you back."

There were tears in Hope's eyes when she hugged her friend goodbye. "Thank you for everything. I'll text you when I'm home."

Monroe gave her arm a final squeeze and stepped out of the way. "Safe travels."

Hope wiped her eyes after she pulled on her seatbelt. She never thought that she'd be heading home after graduation, but now she couldn't wait to get there.

More than one friend had questioned Hope's sanity in agreeing to move.

"What if things don't work out?" her friend Rheese asked.

"Then I'll move back to the city. It's not like I'm moving across the country."

"Are you sure it's a good idea to drop everything for a guy?" Maggie asked.

"That's just it. I'm not dropping anything. I start recording songs next week. And we're already talking about next year's tour."

Hope wasn't giving any of her dreams up. Her career

was skyrocketing. The only thing Hope was risking was her heart. Her past had taught her that love had no guarantees, but Silas and Sierra were the future she wanted. She'd do a lot more than move a few hours away to make sure they had their best chance.

SILAS WAS WAITING in the driveway when she pulled up to the ranch. Sierra stood by his side, her hand firmly clasping his.

Seeing them side by side sent a wave of joy through Hope's body. This was why she was moving home.

"Hope," Sierra called, running to Hope's side as soon as the door was opened. "I missed you."

"I missed you, too. How was school today?" Hope hugged Sierra tightly to her chest.

Sierra held out her knee. "I got a scrape on the playground, but Dad gave me ice cream."

Hope raised her eyebrows at Silas, laughing when he shrugged.

"She was brave," he said. He came around the side of the car, leaning in to kiss her over Sierra's head. "Welcome back."

A chorus of whoops surrounded them. Hope pulled back, shaking her head at her siblings who had filed onto the porch.

"Nice to see you guys, too," she called, grinning as they thundered down the steps.

Thomas was the first to greet her, wrapping her in a hug. "It's good to have you home, Sis."

Each hug that followed reminded Hope that she was where she was meant to be.

It didn't take long to bring Hope's boxes inside. She was carrying the last one up the stairs when Bree ran into the room.

"Hey, Silas. Can I borrow Sierra for a minute?"

Hope glanced at her sister. Bree always seemed to be up to some sort of mischief.

Silas seemed just as confused as she was. "Uh, sure. Pumpkin, do you want to go with Bree?"

Sierra nodded her head and reached for Bree's hand. Hope had no doubt that her family would accept Silas and Sierra into their lives, but it still felt good to see them taking care of her.

Bree and Sierra's laughter faded away, and Hope remembered that she was alone with Silas for the first time since pulling into the driveway. The not so subtle kick to close the door behind them told her that he had realized it, too.

It took less than a second for Hope to wrap her arms around him, tilting her lips up to meet his mouth. There was no need for words as Silas showed Hope exactly how happy he was to see her.

When they broke apart, Hope could feel the flush in her cheeks. "I can't believe I get to do that all the time," she said. "I think I can get used to this."

"I hope so, because I plan on taking full advantage of

every quiet minute together." Silas cocked his head to the side. "Did your sister just steal my daughter away so I could kiss you?"

Hope held a hand up to cover her smile. "It's Bree. I'm guessing she probably did."

Silas's laughter filled the room. "Remind me to tell her that she's my favorite of your sisters."

Hope winked. "You know, she's my favorite, too." She slid her hand up Silas's chest to rest it above his heart.

"Are you really sure about being here?" Silas asked. He covered her hand with his, giving a gentle squeeze.

"I'm sure about being with you." Hope leaned against his chest, tucking her head under his chin.

The arms that wrapped around her were strong and steady. Hope closed her eyes, focusing on the soft fabric against her cheek. She let herself relax into his embrace, knowing that her heart was exactly where she wanted it to be.

CHAPTER 24

Two months had passed since Hope moved back to Elk Mountain, but to Silas, the time had flown by. He couldn't believe how natural it felt to be dating her. They both had worried about resistance from Sierra initially, but Sierra adored Hope. She was constantly asking to go to the ranch to visit.

Work had been gracious in letting Silas switch to a remote, full-time position. He had thought he'd need to find another job, but everyone at work knew how sick Sierra had been. His co-workers were thrilled that she was doing better, even if it meant that they'd see Silas less often.

There had been no more major stomach aches since Sierra's surgery. Silas wasn't naive enough to believe that she would have healed on her own without medical intervention, but he recognized that she was thriving in the country.

Silas recognized that being home had done wonders to help heal his own pain from the past. He had driven a wedge between himself and his family when he left during high school. They had tried to reach out over the years, but Silas hadn't been willing to let them in.

Now, he could see how his own stubborn nature had made his life so much harder than it needed to be. He could dwell on his mistakes from the past, or he could forgive himself and try to do better.

Hope was a huge part of his healing process. She radiated love wherever she went, and Silas counted himself lucky to be surrounded by that glow. When she said she forgave him for hurting her, she meant it. They were forging a future relationship, without the chains from the past holding them down.

There were a few things that hadn't changed over the years. Hope still made Silas's stomach do excited flips whenever she was near. Every kiss sent sparks flying through his body. He couldn't get enough of her.

There were very few things Silas was certain of, but loving Hope was an easy one. He'd happily spend every day of forever with her, if she'd let him. She belonged in his world with him and Sierra.

Summer passed, giving way to the unpredictable weather of fall. Brisk mornings were followed by warm afternoons, but Silas knew it was just a matter of time before the land was gripped in the icy cold of winter.

He and Hope had started taking turns for who planned their dates. Sometimes they brought Sierra along, and sometimes it was just the two of them. Every date left Silas wanting more time with Hope.

It was Silas's turn to plan a date, and he had the perfect activity in mind. He woke up early, his stomach tied in a frenzied knot. He helped Sierra with her jacket while she yawned. It was still dark outside, but the sun would be rising soon. The weather had turned particularly cold that night but that wasn't enough to deter Silas's plans.

"Are you ready to go to the ranch?"

Sierra's face lit up. "Do I get to see Hope?"

Silas tweaked her nose. "She can't wait to give you a hug."

He drove through the streets, each turn taking him closer to the ranch. It had been a couple of days since Silas had taken Hope out and he couldn't wait to hold her in his arms. He hoped the surprise he had planned for her would be worth the early hour.

Hope greeted them at the door, her eyes twinkling when she invited them in. She pulled Silas close, brushing his lips with a kiss before she knelt down to hug Sierra. "How's my favorite girl today?"

Sierra pulled off her scarf. "Daddy says I get to help your mom with chores."

"Oh really? That should be fun." Hope winked at Silas.

"Yeah. I asked her to watch Sierra so we could have some time together before we go to the park."

Mom Matthews came into the room, holding a dish towel in her hands. "You're here!" She hugged Sierra. "Are you ready to be my best helper today?"

"Do we get to see the horses?"

"I was thinking we could make breakfast first. Then we can."

"Yay!" Sierra took her hand, turning to wave over her shoulder before disappearing with Mom Matthews down the hall.

"You know, I don't think I've ever seen anyone that excited about chores." Hope rubbed her chin. "I know I never was."

Silas pulled Hope's coat off a hook on the wall. He held it out for her while she slipped her arms in. "I imagine it's more fun when you haven't been doing them practically since the day you could walk."

"Good point." Hope turned to face Silas, and his breath caught. He couldn't believe the beautiful woman standing in front of him had actually chosen him.

He handed her a scarf and her hat, waiting patiently for Hope to bundle up. She slipped on the hat and lifted her eyes to his. "How do I look?"

The hat was bright pink, with a poof ball on the top that covered half her head. On anyone else, it would look ridiculous, but it fit her personality.

"You look perfect." He kissed each cheek before moving

to her lips. A few kisses later, he pulled back. "Are you ready to go?"

Hope nodded, and took his arm. "Where are we headed?"

Silas pushed down the flutters in his stomach. "It's a surprise."

He led her out the door, turning away from where his car was parked as he pulled a flashlight out of his pocket. Hope raised her eyebrows but didn't say anything. Instead, she let Silas pull her along.

Silas shone the light along the path, looking for the trail that branched off towards the fields. He gripped her hand as he led her through the short grass. Cool air blew in gusts around them and they pulled their jackets close.

"Remind me why we're walking through a field when we could be sleeping in our warm beds?" Hope asked.

Silas tugged the scarf across her neck. "Like I told you, it's a surprise."

Hope looked at his face when he ducked under a fence, a knowing smile dancing along her lips when he held his hand out to her.

"This feels familiar to me."

Silas grinned. "I thought it might." He crossed his fingers, praying that Thomas and Hazel had left everything in place the night before like he requested.

A large tree loomed ahead in the distance, the tall branches barely visible against the dark sky. Silas was confused by the soft glow coming from the platform.

Hope gave his hand a squeeze. "You know, I thought we

were trying to find all the old places we used to sneak away to. We've already been to this one."

"That's true. I thought about finding somewhere else to go, but this spot has the best view."

Silas pulled Hope to the base of the tree, placing his hands on her hips as she climbed up. She paused before stepping onto the platform, looking down at Silas's face.

"What did you do?"

Silas climbed up beside her. Thomas and Hazel had outdone themselves. Instead of only leaving a pile of warm blankets and a couple of large throw pillows, they had scattered the platform with rose petals. Plastic candles lined the edge of the platform, their battery lights flickering in the dark.

A small basket sat near the pile of blankets. Silas lifted the edge, smiling when he saw two insulated mugs. He pulled one out, handing it to Hope. He took a sip from his own mug, only mildly surprised when scalding hot cocoa hit his taste buds.

"How did you pull this off?" Hope's eyes were full of wonder. She cupped the mug in her hands.

"I had a little help." Silas wondered what time Thomas and Hazel had woken up to be able to set up the romantic scene. His heart was swollen with gratitude.

"It's magical."

Silas sat on the pile of pillows, pulling Hope down beside him. He reached for a blanket, wrapping it around their shoulders. He threw another one across their legs. "Are you warm enough?"

She nodded and pulled her knees in, curling up next to his side. Silas wrapped an arm around her shoulders, pressing a kiss to the top of her head while the top of her hat tickled his nose.

Hope looked up at his face. "Do you ever pinch yourself?"

"What do you mean?" It was a strange question.

"To see if you're awake? I keep telling myself that this is my life, but then you do something else that makes me wonder if I'm dreaming. It's all too perfect."

"I know how you feel." Silas adjusted the blanket around her shoulders where it was slipping off. "I don't pinch myself, but I should."

He looked out to the horizon, pointing at the faintest streaks of light that were beginning to appear. "Look."

Hope let out a contented sigh. "I can't even think of the last time I watched the sun come up. I used to see it all the time when I was still living at home."

"I haven't watched it for a long time, either, but I thought it was fitting." Silas studied the side of Hope's face as she turned in the faint light to meet his eyes.

"Fitting for what?" She turned her face back to the horizon.

"The sunrise is the start to a new day. It doesn't seem to matter how many mistakes were made the day before. Each sunrise is a chance to change something, or try to be a little better."

He took a sip of his cocoa. "I made so many mistakes

the first time we were together. I never imagined that we'd be sitting here, side by side, getting another chance."

Hope shifted her weight so that her legs crossed over his. "It's hard to believe that one of the worst moments in my life led to one of my best. I thought my life was ruined when I broke my arm."

"And now you're on the way to being a huge star. I keep waiting for you to remember that you are too cool to talk to me."

Tendrils of orange light branched against the sky, pushing the darkness away. Before long, the sun crested over the top of the mountains.

Silas and Hope watched the sky grow brighter as the sun cast rays through to the valley below.

"Keep planning dates like this, and I'll make sure to always fit you into my schedule."

Silas tried to tickle Hope, but the blankets were in the way. She shrieked anyway, dodging his hands.

"So what I'm hearing is that every date needs to top this one?"

"Absolutely." Hope's laughter was light, but she grew serious. "In all seriousness, though, I like everything we do together." She slid her hand through his. "Even if it means waking up far too early in the morning. I mean, what kind of people actually enjoy being up at this hour?"

"No one comes to mind, except maybe your family." He kissed the top of her head while she laughed.

"Yeah. Except for those silly people who keep the ranch going."

Silas was reminded that Hope had come back to live with her family because of him. "How do you feel about being back home? Do you miss the city?"

Hope leaned her head against Silas's shoulder. "Sometimes. I miss my friends for sure, but I don't want to move back. Not when the person I'd miss the most is right here."

Silas soaked in her words. "I wonder how many times our paths crossed in the city. I mean, I know we lived on different sides of town, so it makes sense that we didn't end up at the same grocery stores, but do you think we ever drove past each other?"

Hope grinned up at him. "Probably at least a couple of times. It's wild to me that we didn't reconnect until we were both in pain."

"It just goes to show that the Lord knows what he's doing far better than I do. I thought Sierra would be sick forever, but I'm not sure I would have brought her home if I hadn't seen you in the office. It was enough of a jolt to break through my stubborn pride and allow me to let my family back in."

Hope sighed. "I hadn't realized how much of the past I was holding on to until I heard your voice. In a strange way, I needed closure before I could open my heart fully. I had no idea that the person I opened my heart to again would be you."

The sun was continuing to rise, making it easier and easier to see Hope's face. Silas slid his hand into his coat pocket, his fingers wrapping around a small object. He pulled it out, careful to keep it wrapped in his hand.

"I've missed too many sunrises without you by my side. I don't want to make that mistake ever again." He lifted Hope's chin, studying every detail of her face, from the curve in her lips to the light in her eyes.

"I can't promise that a life with me will only have beautiful sunrises like the one today. In fact, I can guarantee that we'll see our fair share of rain clouds and stormy skies. What I can promise you is that I will be by your side, with a jacket or an umbrella, to face each day together."

Silas tucked a strand of hair behind her ear. "Do you want to be by my side? Will you share every new day with me?"

He opened his hand, holding out a sparkling silver band. "Hope Matthews, will you marry me?"

She reached up to cup Silas's cheeks with both hands, pressing her forehead to his. "I can't think of anyone I'd rather face each new day with. Yes, I'll marry you."

The sun was high in the sky before Silas and Hope made their way off the platform. Kisses and promises were exchanged in the middle of the clearing, with only the trees listening in, but Silas locked them away in his heart. His happily ever after was about to begin.

EPILOGUE

Three Months Later

Snow blew in sideways gusts as Hope ducked her head and pushed into the barn. She lowered her hood and stood, her mouth gaping open, while she studied the space in front of her.

The barn had been completely remodeled years ago into a large, open area with a couple of rooms jutting off to the side. They used the space for extended family gatherings when there were too many people to comfortably fit in the main house.

Seemingly overnight, the rustic space had been completely transformed into a romantic scene worthy of a movie set. Rows of chairs lined either side of an aisle. Each chair was wrapped with a soft tulle ribbon, knotted to hold a sprig of pink and white flowers. An archway stood at the end of the aisle, with matching flowers and ribbons cascading through the lattice to form a breathtaking backdrop.

Strands of white lights criss-crossed back and forth across the ceiling, casting the room in a soft glow. This wasn't the first party ever to be held at the barn, but Hope knew, without a doubt, it would be her favorite.

She didn't notice her mom coming to stand beside her until she reached for her hand. "Are you ready for this?"

Hope dabbed at her eyes, grateful she hadn't put on her makeup yet. "It's so much better than I ever imagined. Thank you, Mom. I know this was a lot of work."

"It was worth it. I'm so happy for you."

The door to the barn flew open and Bree stepped inside, stomping her boots. "I know February is supposed to be cold, but you sure picked a snowy day for your wedding."

Hope laughed. "I wasn't exactly looking at the weather report when I chose the date."

If Hope had her way, she would have run off with Silas the day he proposed, tying the knot in a courthouse. He was the one who convinced her that they could wait a few months until they could pull together a small wedding.

She followed her mom and Bree to the staircase that led to the loft. They had transformed one of the rooms into a bridal suite. A white dresser sat at one end of the room, filled with makeup and hair products. Another wall held a full-length mirror.

Hope's dress hung from a hook in the corner. Delicate lace cascaded down from a sweetheart neckline, swirling around the bodice to sweep into a full skirt. Teal blue dresses hung on a rack beside it. A smaller white dress hung at the end of the rack, with lace that matched the trim on Hope's dress.

Hope sank to the chair, letting her sister get to work on her hair while her mom steamed her dress.

"How are classes going?" Hope asked.

"My professors are all great, but I don't think high school really prepared me for college. I'm having to learn how to study again."

Hope closed her eyes and tried to calm her nerves while she listened to her sister talk. She was glad Bree was finally at college with their brothers. Finn and Wyatt had driven Bree home for the wedding. The twins were more than happy to take the weekend off, but their brother Hudson was a different story.

Instead of being happy for her, Hudson had grumbled something about having to miss an important event. He had shown up the night before, when the family was heading off to bed, and went straight to his room without so much as a hello.

Hope tried to not take it personally. She and Hudson had been close at one time, but now he was driving a wedge between her and the rest of the family. It was difficult to understand why, when he was constantly shutting them out. At least he had shown up, and no matter how he grumbled, she knew he was there because she asked.

The sound of footsteps on the stairs had Hope's eyes

snapping open. "The guys know to go to the other side of the barn to get ready, right?"

Mom Matthews hurried out the door to check, closing it behind her with a soft click. Hope could hear Silas's voice rising and falling before her mom stepped back into the room, holding Sierra's hand.

"Look who I found." She brushed a hand down Sierra's cheek. "Are you excited for today?"

"Yes!" Sierra's eyes shone bright.

"How's my sweetest girl?" Hope asked, kneeling down so Sierra could run into her arms. "Are you nervous?"

Sierra was going to be the flower girl, and she had been practicing her walk for the past few weeks. She giggled when Hope tickled her side.

"She's not nervous," Bree said. "Right?"

"Right." Sierra beamed up at Bree before climbing onto Hope's lap.

"She's almost done with my hair, and then it's your turn." Hope wrapped her arms around Sierra, fighting back another wave of tears. It didn't seem real that she was about to marry the man of her dreams, and gain this sweet girl as a bonus.

Over the next hour, the room began to fill with her bridesmaids. Hope looked up from the mascara her mom was applying when Emily approached.

"Did you have to get married when I'm as big as a whale?" Emily's eyes sparkled while she held a hand over her very pregnant belly.

"That's my grandchild in there," Mom Matthews said. "You look beautiful."

"I agree. You look gorgeous." Hope hugged her sister-in-law. The baby was due in six weeks, and Hope couldn't wait to meet him.

"So do you." Emily cleared her throat and the room fell silent. "We all wanted to get you a gift." She held out a box.

Hope's hands trembled when she reached for it. Inside the box were six spiral hair pins, each topped with a pale blue gem.

"They are beautiful," she said.

"It's one for each of us," Hazel said. "We want you to know that your sisters are all standing behind you. We love you."

Hope's eyes brimmed with tears as she looked into each of their faces. She had grown up with just one sister, but her collection of sister-in-laws was steadily growing.

Rose reached for the box. "Would you like some help putting them in?"

"Thanks, Rose." Hope dabbed at her eyes with a tissue. "You aren't supposed to be making me cry before I see your brother."

"Didn't you guys already do your bridal photos?" Mia teased.

"Yes, but it's not the same. Today is the day I get to officially become his wife."

Rose twisted the final clip into Hope's curls, right above the line where the veil would rest. She gave her a hug. "It's going to be a beautiful day. Soak in every moment."

"Thanks, Rose." Hope squeezed her hands. "I can't wait to officially become a Foster."

A few minutes later she was surrounded by a sea of blue while the women helped Hope slip into her wedding dress, flouncing the train and making sure every button was in place.

"You look like a princess," Sierra said, her eyes going wide.

"So do you." Hope smiled as Sierra spun in a circle, the white dress fanning out around her. She reached for a teal sash, tying it in a pretty bow around Sierra's waist. "We can both be princesses today."

Hope walked to the full length mirror, marveling at the woman she had been transformed into. She was slowly swaying from side to side when her mom cleared her throat. "It's almost time. Is everyone ready?"

There was a final flurry of makeup touch-ups, and the sisters left the room, Bree holding Sierra's hand.

Hope looked at her mom as the room emptied, her heart filling with emotion. Mom Matthews crossed to her side, lifting up the veil from a stand on the table.

"Ready for the final piece?"

Hope nodded, not trusting herself to speak as her mom clipped the long veil into her hair.

"You are a beautiful bride," she said. "I'm so incredibly proud of the woman you've become."

"Thanks, Mom." Hope gave her another hug and then straightened up. "Ready to walk me down the aisle?"

The next couple of minutes were a blur as Hope joined

the women behind a partition that separated them from the audience's view. Rose handed Sierra her flower girl basket and Sierra disappeared around the partition as strains of a string quartet began to play.

Hope looked across to her row of brothers, lined up behind their own partition. They looked dapper, with their white jeans and button-up shirts and their turquoise vests. Each of them wore a white cowboy hat, bought just for the occasion. It wouldn't be long until those hats picked up dust from the ranch, but for today, they were pristine.

Hudson tipped his hat at Hope before holding his arm out to escort Bree down the aisle. The gruffness from the day before was replaced by a loving smile. Finn and Wyatt were next, nudging each other back and forth until Porter clamped his hands down on their shoulders. They gave Hope a sheepish grin before holding their arms out for Mia.

Rose and Keaton were next, followed by Reid and Millie.

Hazel gave Hope's hand a squeeze before she joined Thomas's side. The nerves kicked up when only Emily and Porter remained. This was it. As soon as they rounded the corner, it would be Hope's turn.

She gave her mom a final hug before taking a deep breath. Then she stepped into the aisle. Her eyes went straight to Silas, standing in front of the arch in a white suit. His eyes held hers, and it was all she could do to keep walking slowly to the beat of the music. She wanted to run into his arms.

The world slowed when Silas reached for her hands,

clasping them in his. "You are exquisite," he whispered, before turning his attention to the pastor.

Hope and Silas said their vows before they exchanged rings. Then they called Sierra up and presented her with a bracelet. Hope's heart overflowed with love as she held hands with the two people who were now her family.

After the ceremony, the chairs were moved to the side while people reached for refreshments. Hope and Silas had both wanted a small ceremony, so the room was filled with only their closest friends and family.

Laughter filled the room as the center of the barn turned into a dance floor. Hope and Silas were talking to Monroe and Felicity when Hudson reached out to tap her shoulder.

"Can I steal you for a minute?"

Silas relinquished her hand and Hudson led her onto the dance floor.

"Thanks for coming." She hated the tension between them. "I wasn't sure you would."

Hudson ducked his head. "I deserve that." He turned her in a slow circle. "I'm sorry I wasn't supportive when you called. I've been working through some things."

Hope lifted her eyes to study her brother's face. "You know the family all loves you, right? It seems like all you do lately is push us away."

Pain flashed across his face, but he quickly schooled his features. "It's more complicated than that."

"Is it?" Hope shook her head in frustration. "What about forgiveness? I'm standing here today, happier than I've ever been in my life, because I was willing to forgive Silas. What did the family do to you that is so bad, you can't forgive us?"

She could hear the pleading in her voice. It hurt to have a rift in the family.

Hudson took a deep breath and blew it out slowly. "I didn't come here to fight, Hope. I'd love to talk about things, but not now. Not on your wedding day." He blew out another breath. "I came to tell you how proud I am of you. I know I'm your older brother, but you've always acted like the older sister to me. You make me proud to know you."

The words were surprisingly sentimental coming from Hudson. Hope dabbed at her eyes. "Thanks. For what it's worth, I'm proud of you, too. You're out chasing your dreams, just like I am. I hope you can find happiness."

"Me too." Hudson spun Hope in a final circle and then handed her off to Porter.

"Thanks, brother." Porter turned his attention to Hope. "You really like to win, don't you?"

"What do you mean?" Hope was confused.

"I mean, with your vows to Silas, you've officially beat Emily and I out. Sierra is now the first grandchild in this family."

Hope held a hand to her mouth. "I didn't even think about that."

He grinned. "Emily and I talked about it. We can't wait for our little guy to have a cousin to play with. If someone was going to beat us to the punch, we're thrilled it's Sierra."

Happiness settled into the center of Hope's heart. She looked over her shoulder to find the little girl who was now part of her world.

Sierra was running in circles, getting chased around the barn by Lacy and Chrissy. Joy filled her face.

"I'm happy it's Sierra, too. Although, if you want to be technical, Sierra is the first granddaughter. You're still going to have the first grandson."

Porter pumped his fist in the air. "Yeah we are."

Hope shook her head, laughing as Silas stepped to her side.

"Can I have my wife back?" he asked.

Porter hugged Hope before making his way over to Emily.

Silas clasped both of her hands, bringing them to his lips. "I like the sound of that word. You're my wife."

"And you're my husband." Her cheeks hurt from smiling so much. She leaned against his chest, closing her eyes to find his heartbeat amidst the laughter of the crowd.

Silas gently swayed from side to side before he pressed a kiss to the top of her head. "Can I show you something?"

Hope nodded, and together, they slipped to the side of the barn. Silas headed for the staircase, pausing on the first step. He reached for her hand, pressing her fingers to the underside of the railing where the wood was rough.

Hope didn't need to see the wood to know what was etched there. H + S.

Hope grinned and pulled him close. "Vandalizing the family barn?"

He winked. "I'll replace the railing if anyone objects. For now, I want it to serve as a secret reminder of our special day."

Hope slid a hand up his chest. "This isn't a day I'll ever forget. I love you, Silas."

He closed the gap between them, lifting a hand to brush the hair behind her ear. "I love you, too."

Millie poked her head around the partition. "If you two sweethearts are done hiding, there's a cake that needs to be cut."

Hope rolled her eyes. "I can't wait to boss you around at your wedding in a couple of months."

"Nothing would make me happier. Just make sure you give Reid a hard time, too. He's already insufferable, counting down the days." She ducked back into the main room, leaving Hope alone with Silas.

Hope stood on her toes to kiss Silas's cheek. She leaned her forehead against his, soaking in the moment before they joined their loved ones.

They had a lifetime of memories to make, and this was just the beginning.

* * *

THE FAMILY SAGA will continue in A Curveball for the Cowboy, coming Spring 2024.

. . .

For more cowboys, check out The Rosecrown Ranch series.

Enjoy the stories of Rosecrown Ranch, where the bonds of friendship and family unfold under a gorgeous Montana sky.

Love at Rosecrown Ranch - She's trading her high heels for cowgirl boots. And maybe, her cheating ex for a handsome man in a cowboy hat.

Longing for Rosecrown Ranch - Can an impulsive city slicker and a hard working cowboy find common ground at Rosecrown Ranch?

Leaving Rosecrown Ranch - He delivered the worst news of her life. Now she has to see him every day. When they are forced to work together at the ranch, will grudges from the past be too hard to overcome?

Download the Rosecrown Ranch collection today and immerse yourself in the picturesque settings and unforgettable cowboys of this clean romance series sure to leave you swooning.

ALSO BY RUTH PENDLETON

Christmas Cheer

The Merry Mishap

The Santa Swap

The Tinsel Takedown

* * *

Elk Mountain Ranch

A Llama for the Cowboy

A Checkup for the Cowboy

A Passing Grade for the Cowboy

A Secret Sunrise for the Cowgirl

A Curveball for the Cowboy

Rosecrown Ranch

Love at Rosecrown Ranch

Longing for Rosecrown Ranch

Leaving Rosecrown Ranch

Made in the USA
Las Vegas, NV
29 January 2024